VIRGINIA BURDON has ha
journalism and publishing, to bro
In between she spent seven years
and working on the edge of one of
More recently she completed a second degree in Fine Arts at London's City and Guilds Art College.

Stalker: A Wall of Silence was inspired by an encounter with a teacher from her school days in New Zealand.

Virginia lives in South West London.

STALKER
A WALL OF SILENCE

VIRGINIA BURDON

SilverWood

Published in 2022 by SilverWood Books

SilverWood Books Ltd
14 Small Street, Bristol, BS1 1DE, United Kingdom
www.silverwoodbooks.co.uk

Copyright © Virginia Burdon 2022

The right of Virginia Burdon to be identified as the author of this
work has been asserted in accordance with the Copyright,
Designs and Patents Act 1988 Sections 77 and 78.

All rights reserved. No part of this publication may be reproduced,
stored in a retrieval system, or transmitted in any form or by any means,
electronic, mechanical, photocopying, recording or otherwise,
without prior permission of the copyright holder.

This is a work of fiction. Names, characters, places and incidents
either are products of the author's imagination or are used fictitiously.
Any resemblance to actual events or locales or persons,
living or dead, is entirely coincidental.

This work is a blend of memoir, fact and fiction, inspired by real events.

ISBN 978-1-80042-215-5 (paperback)

British Library Cataloguing in Publication Data
A CIP catalogue record for this book is
available from the British Library

Page design and typesetting by SilverWood Books

For Tom and Amelia

CHAPTER ONE

The Teacher

It is my first lesson with the new piano teacher. I am twelve years old. I live in New Zealand. It is 1956. I don't know yet who I am. I don't know who she is. I am about to start finding out.

I knock at the door of a small building that looks like a gardening shed. It's the last in a row of buildings that are little more than glorified huts, virtually identical. They are the school piano buildings – eight of them all told. Each one has a narrow pitched roof, its own door, and two windows, one in front, one at the back. Inside there is room for a piano and piano stool. The two used for giving lessons have a second chair for the teacher and their pianos are superior.

Opposite the music huts and next door to the school kitchen is the dining hall. Behind it a hedge of dark green laurels backs onto the public footpath that marks the school boundary. On the other side of the yard intimate laundry flaps lazily in the wind on two revolving clotheslines.

Excitement is high. Girls often choose to wash their underwear themselves rather than risk it to the school's weekly laundry service, but recently a man has been arrested after making nightly forays with his cigarette lighter. The school gates are not secure and he had been zealously burning out the crutches of the underpants until caught by waiting police who mounted a stakeout at the school's request.

Peeping Toms are a more familiar hazard. Like the one I saw last night, peering through the window as I had my bath, his blue-tinged face and hungry eyes pressed up against the glass. My friend says she saw him when she was in the bath too, the same face, the same mad stare before he ducked out of sight and disappeared into the night, furtive as a rat.

When classes are over for the day the air outside the music rooms reverberates with the jumbled cacophony of girls practising. *Fur Elise* competes with *Scenes of Childhood* and scales collide as they bang up and down in opposite directions. If the girls don't turn up for their practise slots they get a demerit. Not long ago I didn't know what a demerit was. There are also merits, and reports, which are serious and the worst of all.

The door opens to reveal the new teacher. The overwhelming impression is of apricot – apricot skirt, apricot blouse, apricot eyebrows. She smells of the dusty powder that clings to her cheeks like a film, masking the rouge beneath. Her long skirt hangs off her hips like a curtain and pale scarves loop her neck below the apricot hair that skims her ear lobes. Then she speaks and introduces herself. She has an English accent and blue eyes. She says her name is Miss Verne. Miss Julia Verne.

She also says my hair is beautiful. I don't know how to respond so duck my head and say nothing. My old teacher never said anything like that. My old teacher wore high-necked silk blouses and buttoned-up cardigans that lay flat across her pinched spinster's chest. She looked more like a nun than a woman and spoke only when she had to. The walls of the music room add to my confusion. Everywhere there are postcards. They seem to be of distant, faraway places. None of them are from New Zealand.

There are also the programmes, some yellowed and dog-eared, pinned up on the wall facing the door. The same name is on every one of them. I've never heard of it – Benjamin Britten. The photograph in the middle shows a face in three quarter view with sharp quizzical eyes like currants, a long nose leading down to a receding chin, and crinkled black hair with a hairline that dips over the centre of his forehead. This man is not attractive. He looks middle-aged, like my mother and father. Besides, isn't a chin like that a sign of weakness? Then I look at the teacher. Her eyes are turned inward and she is flushed with some emotion I cannot interpret. She notices me looking at the walls, and switches her attention back with a visible effort.

'You see all those programmes?' she asks. Her voice is high, almost girlish. It sounds overly refined, genteel even. I think she must be about thirty-five. I can't tell for sure. I'm still at that stage when any adult over thirty looks old, almost as old as my parents.

'I've been to every one of those performances,' she continues. 'I've watched him conduct in six opera houses, I've spent countless hours listening to every one of his recordings.' She pauses, looks away. I realise how tall and thin she is.

'I've studied every musical score, recognized every note for its intention. I've anticipated every musical development and each time I've known exactly what he will say. I know him better than I know myself.'

She doesn't seem to expect a reply, and I don't know if she is telling the truth or not. I think she must be exaggerating. It sounds like a speech she has repeated to herself many times. She wants an audience, and for some reason she's chosen me.

It is all confusing, and embarrassing. I am only twelve, I have red hair, my father is a sheep farmer, and I am a boarder at a girls' school where I am unhappy and feel out of place. Girls my age hate to be embarrassed – ever. Why is she talking like this? She watches me intently, as if to gauge my reaction, and again reaches out a hand to touch my hair. Titian, she repeats, the colour of the Pre-Raphaelites. I don't know what she is talking about. I lack the skills to deal with the situation.

I sit down at the piano and she asks me to play some scales. Much later I'll look back on this moment and recognize it as the opening chapter of a mystery that I will one day have to resolve.

But I get ahead of myself. That is far in the future. All I know right now is that I have somehow landed in the orbit of a woman with apricot hair who has seemingly appeared from nowhere, and who is fixated on a composer called Benjamin Britten.

It is my second lesson with her.

I look at the two round pennies balanced on the backs of my hands. It is before the introduction of decimal coinage; they feel as big as saucers. My fingers are arched like claws over the keys, the tendons straining with the effort of keeping the pennies level so they won't slip. Slowly I start once more from middle C, ascending the two octaves note by note. The right hand penny wobbles, but stays. Then back down again to C with the pennies still in place. Arpeggios are even more challenging. The pennies refuse to co-operate, tipping with a clatter onto the keyboard or dropping to the floor as if belittling my best efforts. I wonder what the point is.

I am to learn to play like Ben, she says. Benjamin Britten. She speaks of him in tones of cloying intimacy. The pennies on the backs of my hands will give me Ben's technique, she says. That's how he plays. I am to learn how to go up and down the keyboard, the pennies balanced evenly, my wrists rotating fluently. My thumb must be tucked against my palm as I play the scales and arpeggios so the pennies don't slide off the flattened area behind my knuckles. If I practise enough I will learn to play like Ben does.

The music teacher is pleased. 'I can tell you are sensitive' she says, 'and that you understand me and understand why it is so important to hold your hands like that. They must look like bells. Technique is everything. That's what Ben has. And that's how he holds his hands. Why am I telling you this? Because I can see that you too are special, and I think you alone understand me when I tell you these things.'

Why me, I think bitterly. Why did she have to pick on me.

Her voice lowers when she talks about him, and fills with warmth. The vowels stretch as she lingers on his name, and her face twists with memories, and loneliness. I begin to sense she is seeking to make me a partner in her strange infatuation and a witness to it, and I feel obscurely manipulated, repelled by the way she seems to take for granted a connection I do not recognize or share, which is assumed without my consent. Her manner has a sickly quality and the nakedness of the emotions she wears on her face is starting to make me feel scornful, even superior.

Worst of all, she seems to want to be my friend. How can a child be a friend with an adult, especially if the adult is also their teacher? But she appears determined; at the next lesson she produces a box of chocolates and says they are a special treat for us to share. Us? Nonetheless I do love chocolates, and it's true. They are a treat.

At home we only really get them at Christmas time, and even then I'm usually left with the peppermints, squished in the back where my mother has pinched them to see what's inside. She hates peppermints for some reason, even though there is always a bottle of Crème de Menthe in the sideboard cupboard alongside the bottles of whisky and gin, dry sherry and brandy, and the wine glasses and sherry glasses, and the cut crystal tumblers that were wedding presents. But she loves orange creams and raspberry creams. They happen to be my favourites too, but she always gets to them first.

So the teacher has been clever, and if this is what friendship delivers so be it. I salivate in anticipation, like a dog that's been offered a bone. As my teeth sink into the soft pink interior of my first chocolate I'm already stepping into a double life – one where I have to dissemble to my friends, and to myself. Right now the chocolates are worth it. Her eyes glint when she recognizes my weakness and she offers me another. And then another. But two is enough. A third would amount to a debt rather than a gift and I'm not going to surrender so easily. I may be a child but I'm a person, not a pet.

She plays in a strange way too, throwing her head back like a swan, her shoulders dipping and rising, her hands floating off the keys like dandelion seeds at the end of phrases. When she closes her eyes and bends her body to the music like a tree in the wind she looks absurd. I am still only twelve. She may pretend she wants to be my friend but I can't supply what she is looking for, whatever that is. I already have a sense that neediness means weakness. No one likes weakness, or neediness. No one at all.

Much of the music sounds strange and unfamiliar too. Most music teachers teach beginner's versions of pieces by the great composers, Mozart or Mendelssohn, Schumann, Haydn, Bach. But this woman doesn't hesitate to play music that is different. The chords often clash and the discordant notes upset my ears until they unexpectedly resolve themselves into harmony.

She tells me the music is by Ben, her Ben, the same man who looks down so insistently from the photo on the wall, a frown etched between his eyes as if permanently judging my inadequate skills. Because she always calls him Ben I think she must have known him very well. She plays his Canticle 1 for me, one of her favourites she says, and quotes the text as if in a dream:

> Ev'n like two little bank-divided brooks,
> That wash the pebbles with their wanton stream
> And having raged and searched a thousand nooks

> Meet both at length at silver-breasted Thames
> Where in a greater current they conjoin,
> So I my best beloved's am.[13]

'You must feel the notes up your arms,' she continues, 'from the tips of your fingers, up your wrists all the way to your shoulders, and through to your heart and mind. Only then will you make the notes sing. But first you must acquire the technique – like Ben.' It becomes a recurring mantra.

'If your hands are held like bells the sound will follow. And each bell is commanded by the wrists. If the wrist is not controlled and balanced the bells will not stay, and the notes will sound harsh, and hard. That's why we use the pennies.'

It is time for me to learn some of his pieces, she adds, producing a score with a piano arrangement for a work called *Les Illuminations.* She makes me say it the French way, repeating the title until I get it right. *i·lu·mi·na·syon,* not *-ations.* I am to practise it for my next lesson. A quick glance is enough for me to see the level is too advanced, but my doubts are brushed aside. She is not disposed to waste time on discussions that do not fit her agenda.

Some of her stories are wonderful and even joyful, stories of concerts in far off countries, in cities with names like Vienna, Venice, Salzburg. She seems to have been to so many; she recites the programmes as she leads me through each in turn, telling me about Britten's extraordinary musicianship, the way he conducts with a baton, constantly pushing and stretching the notes, and always the way he plays the piano, his fingers arched like bells, his hands gliding fluently over the key board. The refrain is repeated and repeated, like a compulsion she's helpless to control. I hope she will keep on talking because otherwise I will have to do the penny exercises again. But at the same time I get a sense that I'm listening to fantasies, not facts. The stories are missing something, an essential feeling of lived experience. Place names are reeled off as if taken from a catalogue. Is she telling the truth or sharing a dream?

When I ask her for details she stops talking and her gaze flickers sideways before we return to the score I'm supposed to be learning.

She has other stories too, more believable ones, about music festivals she's travelled to, seeing famous violinists play in London, listening not just to Ben, her Ben, but to other pianists too. Like Arthur Rubenstein, a slip of a man she says, with a cloud of white hair standing up round his head, perched on his seat like an elf on a mushroom, dwarfed by the grand piano he negotiated with such imperious ease, and about the Gods at London's Royal Opera House.

I don't know what she's talking about until she explains. 'It's the name for the cheapest seats right up at the top of the house, up with the gods, where audiences look down on singers on the stage far below, God-like.'

I seem to spend a lot of my time wondering what she's talking about.

'You have to use opera glasses, miniature binoculars, to see the stage properly,' she adds. 'But you can still hear every note the singers deliver, the basses, baritones, tenors, mezzos, sopranos, and every word they utter.' Just like God.

I tell her in reply about how my father took us to hear *La Boheme* in Christchurch the year beforehand, but the theatre there was small, and I could see the stage and the singers easily. I also tell her that I already know *Your Tiny Hand is Frozen* by heart. For years it has been the song he sings in the car on family outings when he is behind the wheel, and for years we have collectively held our breath, wondering what will happen when he reaches for the high C. It's an ambition he has yet to realise.

We have found common ground at last, and a visit to the

Royal Opera House is added to the list of my own ambitions for the future.

It still sounds impossible though, and I cannot stop myself asking how the singers manage to make themselves heard in such a huge space. So I learn about voice training. She puffs out her chest to show me what breath control means, and demonstrates breathing exercises, filling her lungs with air. Disarmingly she laughs at herself and I see that she too was once a girl. The intimacy of the room, with just the two of us, feels like a cocoon where I can join her in a shared respite from reality.

What with this and the chocolates, I start to look forward to the lessons despite my reservations. And if some of her stories are made up I don't care because I'm getting used to having a little bit of each week that is almost my own. The only other times are when I get lost in a book I'm reading, or am on punishment duty. The smallest breaches, like late homework, talking in class, having dirty gym shoes, an unmended ladder in a stocking, a lost panama hat, or talking after lights out, they all lead to punishments, more and more of them, punishments like polishing the chapel floor, cleaning the candle sticks on either side of the altar with Brasso, writing meaningless lines – 'I wandered lonely as a cloud', or route marching in step with a dejected band of other girls who, like me, have also failed to shine their shoes or fix a fallen hem.

Up and down the school driveway we go, up and down, left right, left right, gravel crunching underfoot, back and forth in step, on pointless Sunday afternoons for an hour at a time, come rain or sunshine, watched by a bored prefect who adds extra minutes if we slow down or slacken. Precious minutes I could be spending in the school shrubbery instead, smoking an experimental cigarette made out of dried grasses rolled in lavatory paper, cigarettes that make my throat burn as if it's on fire, or absorbed in the pages of the forbidden women's magazines that are passed around, hand to hand, with their compelling problem pages. Or urging on my paperback heroine Angelique to surrender to her new husband, a devastatingly handsome French count with a sardonic tongue and a magnificent chateau somewhere in eighteenth century France.

I decide to fall in love with blond Angelique myself, and wince when the loyal old nurse plucks out her pubic hairs one by one on the eve of her wedding to a man she hardly knows. No wonder poor Angelique doesn't want to have sex. It's all deeply frustrating, like Scarlett O'Hara and Rhett Butler in *Gone with the Wind*, another of the books that is circulating in my class and which I'll read in secret when it's my turn. Why can't these women just get on with it.

Their dark brooding heroes become a model for the husbands I'm already dreaming about. The teacher is welcome to her Ben with his uncertain chin and crinkled hair. My Rhett is incomparably more handsome and besides, he doesn't give a damn. One day I'll get to read *Lady Chatterley's Lover* too, but I'll find it tame by comparison because by then my curiosity about sex will have become blunted by experience, and the crippled husband's relations with his nurse will seem an altogether more intriguing prospect than Lady C's couplings with rustic Mellors.

Poor Rhett. Little does he know he'll soon be replaced by Ivanhoe, then Sydney Carton of the immortal words, 'It is a far, far better thing that I do than I've ever done.' I envisage Sydney stepping up to the guillotine, his pure white linen shirt collar turned back to expose the perfect neck and lightly tanned throat. Then the whoosh of the falling blade and the thump as it lands, the blood spurting in a crimson fountain as his handsome head drops gracefully into the basket and the wrinkled *tricoteuses* return to their knitting, needles click-clicking away in unison as they wait like vultures for the next victim, maybe the Queen, Marie Antoinette, to take his or her turn.

Sydney's words stir my heart beyond description. They are

even more romantic than the distant prospect of another hero looking deep into my eyes one day from where he is kneeling at my feet, and asking, 'Will you marry me?' a velvet-lined box containing a ring dwarfed by a huge solitaire diamond sitting in the palm of his raised right hand, his left hand with its five perfect fingernails clasped against his heart. If he's left-handed it will be the other way round.

And I'm not sure why, but I seem to get punishments more than anyone else. I don't think of myself as a difficult, or bad child. Other girls are much worse, but they also seem much better at not getting caught. Sometimes I wonder if it's because of my red hair, hair that makes me stand out because it's neither mouse nor blond. Sundays are also the day when we have to write compulsory letters to our parents, but there's really nothing to say. If there were something to say I wouldn't say it in any case. And I would never tell them about my strange new music teacher.

One Sunday I simply put an empty sheet of paper into the envelope, but I am found out by the teacher on duty, and I agree that deserves a punishment, even if it does mean doing flower arrangements for the chapel's Sunday evening service, something I'm extraordinarily bad at. But at other times I'm at a loss, so end up doing bad things to make sense of the punishments because otherwise they make no sense at all. I cut corners in silent protest when I'm on floor-polishing detail and push the piles of dust under a hassock, or spit on the altar cloth wondering if God will decide to punish me instead, and if so how. If he notices me that will be good enough. How else to stand out from the millions and millions of people who think they matter to him too. Besides, doesn't the Bible say God loves a sinner?

But even worse than the exercises with the pennies are the times when she stops telling me how to play and starts going on about my hair again, stroking it while she talks, flicking the odd stray strand out of the way. She keeps on calling the colour titian and saying how beautiful it is, that it makes me special too. But I don't feel special. I just feel deeply uncomfortable, and wish she wouldn't say such things, or touch me like that. Even the chocolates don't make up for the way she puts her hand on my head.

At other times though I feel scared when her mouth sets and her mood changes, when she tells me to move out of the way so she can sit at the piano instead and bang out chords recklessly, sending the noise rampaging around the confines of the hut, the notes bouncing off the yellow fibre-board walls until I have to put my hands over my ears.

CHAPTER 2

The Betrayal

As the weeks pass my feelings about the teacher become confused, and increasingly complicated. I struggle to get a handle on her personality. It seems to be constantly shifting, changing from one lesson to the next. One moment she retreats into herself and looks almost lost as if she doesn't know who she is or what she's doing. The next she's assertive and full of a kind of furious energy.

Is she merely peculiar, or is she instead a natural rebel, someone who is happy to ignore the conventions that separate teachers from their pupils, who acts as if rules are there to be broken, not followed, who treats the metronome that sits on top of the piano with contempt, who breathes *ritardando* as if it were a sigh. Do her odd ways offer an alternative to the constricting norms and the endless regulations that pervade every aspect of the boarding school life that defines my world, the clanging bells announcing hourly lessons, the cramped dormitories with their narrow bunks and mildewed corners, and the rigid rotas for the thrice-weekly bath times? It's impossible to tell, so I fasten on a new word I discover. Iconoclast. An adult word. Like propinquity, deliquescence, transference, psychosis, nemesis, hubris. I relish the sound it makes, the way my tongue is forced to curl around the syllables. Iconoclast. I have a use for it immediately.

Meanwhile the strange disrupted lessons continue and I begin to feel a reluctant sense of responsibility for her. If only she can change her ways and behave more like a normal teacher, perhaps the other girls will start to accept her as an eccentric rather than a freak, and behave better in the class singing lessons.

My father is eccentric and as his children we bask in his reputation. He wears raspberry pink nylon socks after buying three dozen pairs in a sale when he had a minor lottery win, and holds his work trousers up with binder twine salvaged from hay bales, instead of a belt. He reads books in classical Greek by Thucydides or Herodotus when he's on the lavatory. He writes a letter to *The Press* complaining that New Zealand women are ugly and signs himself Adonis, prompting a flood of replies from Aphrodites. And on Christmas day he sings *O Come All Ye Faithful* in Latin at the local church where he and my mother were married, his voice soaring above the surprised congregation.

But in other ways he's normal too, proving you can be both normal and eccentric at the same time. He can swear fluently and shear a sheep, and is an excellent fly fisherman. His drives on the nearby golf course swerve like partridges. He digs the vegetable garden, grumbling about the amount of twitch he has to pull out, and traipses up and down the lawn behind an ancient lawnmower that belches blue two-stroke fumes in his face. He and my mother are avid bridge players and once a week drive thirty miles there and back to the nearest bridge club. And my mother is extremely normal, a leading light in the local Women's Institute and an expert needlewoman, skilled at darning and smocking, at golf and tennis and flower arrangements, and at painting the dimple on empty whisky bottles with roses and foxgloves for turning into lamp bases and selling at the WI bazaar. Above all she is supremely practical, the perfect foil for her husband, my father, who struggles to change a fuse.

Normal teachers clap to get attention and restore order. They earn and command respect. They give out punishments and rewards, they use a blackboard when giving lessons, and they mark homework. Sometimes they get cross. The maths teacher recently threw a wooden blackboard duster at me, aiming for my head. And when he catches me daydreaming and staring out the window the French teacher, a stocky man with blond hair from Germany who looks like Martin Luther, makes me stand on a chair until the lesson is over.

But the one thing they can never reveal is what they really think, or show their real emotions either, because if they do the girls will instantly exploit the weakness this reveals. If my music teacher can only understand this her life will become easier, and I won't have to feel embarrassed on her behalf, or guilty, even though I don't know why I should.

But she just looks helpless when the class singing lessons she has to take veer out of control, and struggles to hide the tears of frustration. Or maybe they're tears of rage and we just don't know it.

As for her passion for Britten, I remain incapable of judging whether this is perverse or not because I am, after all, only a child.

And whenever I think she is becoming more normal she lets me down. Again and again.

The weekly Form 2 singing classes are the worst of all because then she singles me out in front of everyone with sideways glances of naked complicity. As if we were allies. All I want is to be ignored, spared the embarrassment of being exposed as her favourite. Doesn't she know how ridiculous she looks, or realise that *Nymphs and Shepherds* is a joke when her voice warbles like that. She is more embarrassing than anyone else I have ever met, and the embarrassment mortifies me. It is testing my limited loyalty to breaking point.

As the weeks go on the teasing gets worse. 'Teacher's pet,'

my classmates mock, 'teacher's pet. Tell us what she says in your lessons. Is she really as mad as she seems?'

Actually, it's not really teasing, and it's not malicious either. They have been quick to sense I am experiencing something they are excluded from, even though I've not told them about the chocolates, and since most of our experiences are shared ones I don't have the right to an alternative.

We have all had to learn to deal with the collective lack of privacy by embracing collective conventions, and one of them is having a pash, as in passion. In an all-girls' school it is perhaps inevitable that emergent sexual awareness has to find a channel for its expression, and in the sub-culture we belong to by definition, pashes have become the accepted way.

At the age of twelve, peer pressure alone means it's time for me to find my own pash amongst the seniors, but the most assertive third formers have first pick of the alpha possibles, and I am late off the mark. Top ranking contenders are the prefects and those seniors who display coveted red stripes – sashes worn around the waist and awarded for all round excellence, but there is a strict hierarchy and I have limited choices left. The upshot is that I end up with one who is only a monitor, and no red sash at that, not even the distant prospect of one.

Joanna is therefore surprised when I offer her an apple from my weekly fruit order, the accepted form of overture, and looks bewildered before she realises she has just been invited to join the elect. The arrangement is formally cemented when she accepts my meagre offering, even though it's tacitly recognized that neither party has any enthusiasm for the arrangement. It is an institutional necessity, one that links me to my classmates in the same way that the onset of periods does. Settled obligations will require me to send her notes and find out when her birthday is so I can present her with an extra piece of fruit on the day and give her a hand-made card.

The arrangement ends early, withered by tokenism and a shared reluctance to settle for second best. Lindsay S in the B stream has already bagged the head prefect. I want a Rhett instead, a real man, not a mediocrity in uniform like Joanna. Sensible charisma-free Joanna.

As for Lindsay, she never gets the chance to become a pash in turn. Her parents take her out of school as soon as she reaches school-leaving age and within a couple of years she's engaged, then married, to a neighbouring farmer's son, and is soon invisible, buried in babies. I play the harmonium at the wedding which is celebrated in the open air, surrounded by the salt marshes that fringe the family farm and lend the air a tang of iodine. The reception is held in a marquee with billowing awnings that flap in the wind. The best man has to shout over the noise.

One girl who is different and incapable of conforming is Susan H, a tall gangly-limbed girl with fair hair and fathomless deep-set blue eyes, and no discernable talents at all. Susan is inherently friendless, and so peculiar that she defies judgement. Susan regularly tries to get into bed with other girls in her dormitory, clambering up the ladders to the top bunks, all without saying a word as she fumbles for an embrace. We tolerate her because we don't know what else to do. We cannot judge her because we don't have a yardstick to do so, and lack a label. Certainly no one thinks of reporting her, because her behaviour falls outside anything we know about.

So we don't gang up on her, and maybe that's the most extraordinary thing of all. If anything we feel protective towards Susan. Collective loyalty is powerful, and Susan may be a problem, but she is our problem. When her attempts to kiss are rebuffed she returns to her bottom bunk as silently as she left it. Susan never tries to get into bed with me and I feel obscurely left out, offended even. I wonder why not. It's almost like being rejected.

What our teachers cannot realise therefore are the ways in

which these hidden experiences bind us girls together and drive our loyalties to each other – loyalties that are in their way absolute and outside our control, which take precedence over nearly everything else, and for me, over my strange piano teacher who seems incapable of compromise.

So inevitably the day comes when I have to choose between her, or the teasing. And honestly, to be truthful it's no contest.

I prepare carefully.

The weekly singing classes are held in the school hall, a long rectangular building with wooden floors, a high cavernous ceiling, and at one end a raised platform with pretensions to be a stage. Like most school halls it does duty on many fronts. Twice a day, in the morning and evening, prayers are held in compliance with the school's status as an Anglican foundation, and the 150 uniformed girls on the school roll take their places in class order on the rows of benches facing the front. The sixth formers file in last and for a whole term I keep my eyes peeled for the sight of the one I currently yearn for, not Joanna, but Rosemary F with her prominent nose, large thyroid eyes, and flawless complexion. The presiding teacher, usually the head mistress, then enters by a side door and everyone stands up in a collective shuffle. Members of the staff cohort congregate at the rear as she ascends the six steps to the stage and crosses to take her place behind the carved oak lectern.

Pride of place on the stage's right hand side is occupied by the school's grand piano: piano students are assigned by rota to play suitable pieces as the teacher on prayer duty enters and leaves. They also accompany the daily hymns chosen by the head of the music department to chime with the liturgical calendar, avoiding any with too many awkward flats or sharps.

When morning prayers are over the benches are piled back against the walls and the hall resumes its primary function as the school gymnasium. Parallel bars line the side walls, springboards, mats, and the infamous leather 'horse' are dragged out from their storage places in the corners, and the ropes that hang languidly from the lofted ceiling are unlooped so that girls can climb or dangle from them depending on their abilities. Margaret M is the clumsiest, her buried muscles incapable of lifting her weight off the floor, anchored to the spot by the dictates of gravity and obesity. Margaret's dimpled white skin, soft and pale as dough, shows every bruise.

In winter the hall is also used for ballet and ballroom dancing lessons, the girls taking turns to be a man. The teacher is a tiny woman with preposterous posture and an unbending attention to her 'frame'. She tap-taps across the wooden floor in her trademark scarlet shoes with their kitten heels and glistening scarlet straps – head up, bosom out, shoulders back. She affects a pronounced French accent that sits at odds with her English surname and is much given to gesticulation. Her blood-red finger nails gleam like talons.

And once every two years the hall is transformed for the biennial school play. The head of music is an ardent admirer of Gilbert and Sullivan. Working parties are organised to paint the backdrops, and grease paint and burnt corks taken out of storage in cardboard shoeboxes to turn the leading singers and chorus into pirates from Penzance, or courtiers to the Mikado. Cheap fabrics intended to imitate satin or silk are transformed by enthusiastic but inept sewing bees into ill-fitting pirate costumes and kimonos, and hours of practice eat up any remaining spare time before parents are formally invited by post to come and see their daughters masquerading as sailors and D'Oyly Carte professionals, as Nanki-Poo or the Three Little Maids. In a final nod to gender, bass, baritone and tenor parts are recast in keys and octaves to fit the limited range of the girls' fledgling teenage voices.

But on this day, the day I have been planning for, the

hall is being used for the weekly singing lessons, and the class is still learning *Nymphs and Shepherds, Come Away.* Come, come away. The words seem prescient. The teacher is seated at the piano, deflated already by her persistent failure to gain the class's attention and by the usual giggling and whispers. She is not a disciplinarian. Teaching a whole class remains outside her experience and she is aware of her ineptitude. The pleading glance she directs my way, as if seeking my support, seals the decision I've made in secret. I'm going through my late-pubescent religious phase, and the denial of St Peter and Christ's prediction is my model: 'Before the rooster crows, you will disown me three times.'[2]

As the last chord of the first verse dies and she raises her hands, something hard and round drops to the hall's wooden floor and rolls away. She turns to see where the sound has come from. I remain still, seated on a bench near the front between two classmates.

At the beginning of the next verse I drop another marble. The glinting ball of green and white glass rolls away again, rattling loudly as it jumps the cracks between the floorboards. By now everyone has realised what is happening. Again, the teacher pauses and looks around.

When I drop the third marble the class breaks into open sniggers, with all eyes on her to see her reaction. But this time the teacher knows who the culprit is.

She turns again and I force myself to stare back, steeling myself against the recognition and distress on her face as she registers the betrayal. Standing up abruptly, she stumbles from the stage, nearly tripping down the stairs as she leaves, and staggers out the door. My classmates crowd around with congratulations, patting me on the back, laughing, but the moment's tenuous satisfaction has been ruined. The teacher had spoken only three words, 'Not you too.' But she had looked so broken and devastated that I wonder what I have done.

She leaves the school the same day. Afterwards I think about her and where she disappeared to, but only sometimes. Unlike St Peter I don't weep bitterly. Or dwell on regrets. After all, I am still just a child.

CHAPTER 3

Discovery

I now live in Cambridge, England, 12,000 miles and almost thirty years away from that distant boarding school. I have a job I enjoy, and child minders and au pairs for my children. The current one is Tsafra, a psychiatry graduate from Israel who has recently completed two years of mandatory military service. Tsafra makes exquisite salads, slicing every ingredient into the smallest of pieces, delivering a gourmet miracle infused with the exotic herbs she tracks down in the market square.

When Tsafra's year of learning English comes to an end she is replaced by Beatrice from France, a big friendly girl who buys them bubble gum behind my back and compares notes with other au pairs when they meet in town to swap stories about their employers – whether they are expected to do housework on top of childcare duties, to iron shirts or empty litter trays, who has the most time off, how much they are paid, which husbands try to flirt, or worse. The children think she's wonderful.

Our terraced house near Mill Road is within easy cycling distance of the city centre. When we move in the first thing I do is take out the deeply practical new doors with their sand-blasted glass panes and find old ones, combing the local reclamation yards, tracking down men with scarred hands who agree to strip the paint off in acid baths. At the beginning of the second week an elderly man with a friar's pate and a gentle face knocks on my front door saying he is from the council and do I need assistance financially, or in applying for benefits. I must have looked surprised because he explains that he can always tell when people need to go on the benefit, and he is there to help. I don't disabuse him, but wonder whether I should smarten up.

On the corner five houses down there is an Italian delicatessen, a real one, with big-bosomed Mamma presiding behind a counter laden with trays of freshly made pizza and warm bread straight from the oven. Mamma's diminutive husband hovers in the background at her beck and call, fingering his neat black moustache, jumping to attention when ordered. The eldest son, who does most of the baking, is being groomed to take over the business along with his fiancée. When they are killed in a multi-car pile-up while driving back from London late one winter night, Mamma's grief is indescribable and the shop, dimmed by tragedy, is sold soon after.

On the other corner, at a crossroads, there's the Irish pub with a shamrock painted on a board above the entrance. It's the last remaining pub of a cluster of four, built facing each other in the nineteenth century to serve the workers on the railway tracks that converge at the station less than a mile away. I wonder how their families managed to cram into the narrow two-bedroomed cottages that line the street, and think of all the beaten wives and cowering children, waiting for the return of drunken husbands and fathers, fists flexed, belts unbuckled at the ready. I hope I am wrong, but Cambridge's historic support for the temperance movement suggests a red flag.

We also get a cat from the local Blue Cross cats' home. Asterix is black as night, and we soon discover that he hates other cats with a passion. Every morning he does his rounds of the garden, vigorously and conscientiously spraying the bushes. Somehow he manages to do this without losing a shred of his innate dignity. If another cat enters the garden his fur stands on end as he growls and hisses, back arched, and his ears flatten against his head.

Asterix also likes to sleep on my pillow during the day, even though he knows it's forbidden. We are an anthropomorphic household. He clearly thinks that if he leaves my bedroom when I come back from work I won't know he's been there, but the tell tale black hairs on my pillowcase are a sure giveaway. Asterix may be short on intelligence sometimes, and struggle with cause and effect, but he makes up for it with high quality ESP. No matter what time of day or night I return home, he materializes as if by magic as I take out my keys to let myself in at the front door, rubbing a welcome against my legs.

My daughter still yearns for her very own cat however, which is how we come to acquire a small ginger kitten she calls Wonky. Asterix hates Wonky even more than the cats that defecate in the garden so Wonky finds a friendlier household without a resident cat down the road. He also associates our house with the car that hit him one night, leaving him with a broken pelvis and a tail that had to be amputated when it became gangrenous.

After we've taken him back twice we give up. Asterix and Wonky both, I'm sure, breathe a sigh of relief. Wonky's new owners are an elderly couple with watery eyes and antimacassars on the backs of their armchairs. He finds them infinitely preferable, and we leave him kneading the old woman's legs, digging his claws in and out. It must be painful but she's a game old bird and refuses to even flinch. When we say goodbye she is still stroking him firmly as if to emphasize that the transference of ownership is complete. And Wonky is still digging his claws into her shrunken thighs, in and out, in and out, purring noisily.

Away from home I go to the main library for books and CDs, and on summer evenings play tennis on the courts in neighbouring Histon, or golf at Girton. Once a week I drive to a barn outside nearby Cherry Hinton to join an evening life drawing class. At the top of steep wooden stairs a heavy trapdoor opens onto a loft that smells of hay. The models, usually women, but occasionally a man, pose on a chair or lie on cushions, their skin softly lit by covered light bulbs hanging from black extension cords. No one talks. The only sound is the faint scrape of pencil or charcoal on paper, and the rubbing noises erasers make, until the solemn retired architect who arranges the sessions puts his drawing pad down and calls time. Further down the road the county's mental home lurks on the outskirts of the village, a looming Victorian reminder of lost lives and sanatoria, and a dark-eyed medical student called Donald babysits for free. He is a committed Christian who tells me he's never touched alcohol. I wonder what happens when it's his turn to drink from the communion chalice? Does he take a pretend sip only? Or does transubstantiation mean the alcohol is successfully vitiated.

And over time I meet many other people through my work which takes me all over East Anglia. Often they become friends too. I allow get-lost time when I have to drive to Lincolnshire or Leighton Buzzard, or wherever my diary directs me, and am regularly defeated by Peterborough's new ring road. Colchester's is almost as challenging. How did the Romans manage?

So in a thoroughly normal way my life is full. Full enough. Cluttered with work, life in Cambridge, bringing up children, looking after pets, and domestic dramas.

I am not looking for anything more.

I am not on a mission.

Or not until the day I wander over to the biography section in the central library and my eye is caught by a small book about Benjamin Britten. The title triggers a faint memory of the strange music teacher I had in my childhood, and I pick it up out of passing curiosity. It is by one of his librettists, Ronald Duncan, and can be no more than about 50,000 words compressed into a slimmed-down volume of 180 pages. I start skim reading it, my mind scarcely engaged, until I suddenly come upon a paragraph that grabs my full attention. It is about a woman who became convinced she was Britten's wife, and who eventually invaded a performance he was conducting of his opera, *The Turn of the Screw,* at the 1955 Aldeburgh Festival.

I sign the book out with shaking hands, and back in my office take photocopies of pages and pages, anything in fact that is relevant. The book is out of print, and short of never returning it to the library and accepting a fine, this is the best I can think of.

For the chance discovery has opened a floodgate of memories and raised questions that will refuse to go away. In the space of an instant I have been taken back to the distant day when I rolled some marbles across a wooden floor in an act of petty rebellion with unknown consequences. From now on I will be dogged by a growing conviction that the woman in the Duncan memoir and the woman who was my teacher are one and the same person.

But if so, how come she ended up in New Zealand, a place so pre-eminently ill suited to the person I remember from my schooldays? A woman who seemed woefully out of place, and who disappeared without trace.

It is the beginning of a search for an elusive truth that will eventually turn into a story of power and influence, implacable loyalties, unrequited love, and a wall of silence. A search that will not leave me in peace until I have addressed the mystery of who she was, and what became of her.

The book I've found is called *Working with Britten: A Personal Memoir.*

Published by Duncan's own Rebel Press in 1981, it was the final title in a series of autobiographies that were criticised at the time for what was considered their dubious and often controversial opinions and subject matter. The book had already been rejected by a mainstream publisher amid rumours of possible legal problems.

By all accounts Duncan appears to have been a colourful, indeed fanciful character, with a flair for self-aggrandisement and impressive reserves of creative energy – a polymath, essayist, poet, librettist, novelist, scriptwriter, playwright and farmer. After graduating from Cambridge he had a short spell working in a mine near Chesterfield. Later he went briefly to India and met Mahatma Gandhi. He writes that he was '...wholly corrupt by the age of four, and aware of that by the time I was fourteen,'[3] and in one of his autobiographies claims to be the grandson of the last crown prince of Bavaria on the grounds that his father was the prince's illegitimate son.

He was also, like Benjamin Britten, an early pacifist from the mid-1930s, well before the outbreak of the Second World War, and in contact with key figures in the emergent Peace Pledge Union. I am intrigued to note that he also wrote the script for the 1968 film starring Marianne Faithfull, *Girl on a Motorcycle*. A photograph of a bronze bust of him by Jacob Epstein on the book's back cover speaks to his connections.

His relationship with Britten is variously reported to have started with their shared pacifist convictions and a failed project dating from 1938 when he wrote the words for Britten's unsuccessful *Pacifist March*. A few years later he helped Britten with the libretto for the final act of *Peter Grimes*, and in 1946 completed the entire libretto for *The Rape of Lucretia*. Britten in turn contributed the incidental music for three of Duncan's plays.

Although their professional relationship ended in 1951 when Britten declined to write the music for another Duncan project, the two men remained close friends, with Britten staying at the Duncan's Devon home, and joining the family on shared holidays abroad. Duncan and his wife even arranged for Britten to be their two children's guardian should they die.

So all well and good so far, but I learn later on that the Duncan/Britten connection had a darker side, that it eventually expanded to encompass not just Duncan's family but more particularly his son too, raising questions about a tacit acquiescence to the child's inclusion in the succession of young boys who were regularly invited to Britten and Peter Pears' home at Crag House in Aldeburgh, and later the Red House.

The young Roger Duncan first met Britten when he was eleven, and Britten subsequently offered to, in effect, adopt him when the Duncan marriage was in difficulties. The proposed arrangement would allow him to give the boy gifts and have him to stay during the school holidays. Although nothing untoward appears to have happened, eyebrows were raised. Duncan senior remains circumspect in this respect, however, referring towards the end of his book that, 'In these pages I have not revealed all I know of Britten, or all he confessed to me about himself. I will seek the compassion of silence.'

For Britten it all began earlier in the same year when something happened that troubled him deeply. According to Duncan's *Britten* memoir, Britten contacted him with extraordinary news: he had received a proposal of marriage.[4]

Duncan admits that at first he treated Britten's call as amusing rather than as a serious issue, writing in his account that 'I was in a frivolous mood. That's a misfortune which occurs to us all, I said.'[5]

His initial reaction is understandable. Britten was in an established relationship with his partner, the tenor Peter Pears. He had, moreover, acquired a questionable reputation for his fondness for adolescent boys, and while there is no doubt his charismatic personality attracted a certain type of woman, and there were many in his coterie of admirers, he was uncompromisingly homosexual despite it still being illegal at the time.

The two men share a house together and have effectively turned their home into a 'safe space', skilfully navigating the conventions of the day. Some wit has suggested it should be called 'Homo Sweet Homo', and it is an open secret among their circle that they have been lovers since 1939. In his letters to Pears Britten routinely addresses him as 'My darling', 'My darling heart'; ends them with 'How long, how long.' But their professional relationship as performers provides valuable cover and they take the utmost care to be discreet about this incriminating aspect of their personal life. There was that nasty scare in 1953 when Britten received a visit from the police after the then Home Secretary demanded that the Victorian era laws against homosexuality should be enforced, but thankfully no further action was taken.

They still shudder at the memory. Pears even considered a sham marriage.

In other respects Britten is decidedly prudish. He frowns on vulgar or suggestive humour, and breaches of social protocols are judged severely. He has been absorbed into the Establishment. His diction is precise, modulated, upper-received. He sounds excellent on the radio, warm, courteous and convincing, with not a hint of the ruthless streak his so-called corpses, discarded from his inner circle, learn to rue. He is reputed to have an extraordinary talent for listening, for making his interlocutors feel as if they are the only person in the room.

So Duncan tells Britten to frighten the woman off, to call her bluff. She's only doing it to show off to her girlfriends, he says. Besides, 'You're too well known not to run into this sort of thing. But if I were you I'd avoid seeing her. If you did, out of pity, she might even claim you assaulted her.'[6]

But Britten is becoming increasingly worried. He has never to his knowledge even met the woman.

It emerges that she lives in Huddersfield, and he admits that she has already sent him more than a dozen amorous postcards in the run-up to the proposal. He had thought they would stop when he went abroad on tour recently, but now he is back they have started again. She openly declares her love for him and evidently believes he loves her back. How did she get his address? Surely she knows about him and Peter?

Recently he has also sensed that he is being watched through the windows of Crag House, and this makes him even more uneasy. It is time they moved from their seafront home. Last week Peter found fresh graffiti scratched into the chairs in the dining room, people's initials, intruders. Sightseers have been spotted standing on tip-toe, peering over the walls into the garden. It is all becoming intolerable.

In a subsequent phone call to Duncan Britten speaks of his growing anxiety. His initial irritation has turned to alarm. This time it's a letter. Apparently the woman now believes she is his wife and he fears the situation may escalate out of control. The possible consequences are too disquieting to ignore. But what can he do?

He thinks back to the manservant he employed four years beforehand who went literally mad, becoming convinced that he was the composer and demoting Britten to his manservant in turn while he conducted from the grand piano. The portents are already there.

By this point the postcards and letters are no longer coming from Huddersfield but from an address in London's Bayswater district, not far from Sussex Gardens, which at the time has something of a reputation as a red light area. Duncan by now shares Britten's disquiet, so he asks his wife and secretary if they will arrange to meet the woman in person. But when they arrive at the address on the most recent letter they discover it doesn't exist. The Eighth Aldeburgh Festival is due to open in six weeks' time, but neither Duncan nor Britten can begin to anticipate, let alone envisage the events that lie in wait.

Soon it becomes all too apparent. On 19 June, the day after the annual Festival's opening performance of *The Turn of the Screw* at the town's Jubilee Hall, Britten contacts Duncan again in immense distress. The night beforehand one of the very best performances of his opera had been wrecked, he says. The woman claiming to be his wife invaded the theatre by getting in through the stage door and screaming out his name, 'Ben, oh Ben'. Her family intervened and bundled her into a taxi. It took the combined efforts of four people to remove her.

It was all too terrible, he writes to Duncan. Her awful cries echo in his ears.

CHAPTER 4

The Foundation Library

It is now many years since I found the Duncan memoir, but in the interim my quest has become stalled, effectively put on ice. Why? For all the usual reasons – work intervened, work and London, then Cambridge and back to London again, changing jobs, moving house, steering children through exams and university. In short the Duncan account had been sidelined by exigency, by the sheer demands of life.

But the children have now left home and are adults. My free time is once more my own, and I find I cannot stop thinking about the Duncan memoir again. The time has come to return to the mystery of the woman who believed she was Britten's wife, and my own links with a story that has remained a stubborn background constant.

If I don't seize and resolve this opportunity I fear my memories will follow me down the years, keeping me tied to an event from my past that has been reawakened, and which refuses to lie down. Only by finding out more will I be able to make sense of what I have learnt so far and satisfy questions that have never gone away. It's like being stalked by a ghost who won't give up until I've paid my dues.

I decide to go to Aldeburgh in person, to explore the streets, soak up the town's atmosphere, and see the Jubilee Hall where *The Turn of the Screw* was performed. I also need to visit the Britten-Pears Foundation Library as this will surely hold the answers I am seeking.

I was last there in the year of the Mad Cow disease outbreak, in 1986. Bovine spongiform encephalopathy. Jars of beef extract had disappeared from supermarket shelves, butchers were no longer selling oxtail, and local footpaths had been closed to the public to contain the disease's lethal spread while across the country thousands of cattle were being slaughtered by antipodean veterinarians. The clouds of smoke spiraling skyward pinpointed the grim funeral pyres where the carcasses were burning, and ribbons of yellow tape barred stiles and gates to weekend ramblers, forbidding them their customary access to ancient rights of way and bridle paths. Weeping farmers were captured on camera as they watched their prized herds being rounded up for execution. A white bull calf that escaped the awful cull became a mascot for the nation and a symbol of hope for the future.

I spent the weekend with a work colleague at her cottage in neighboring Orford. She was an extremely good squash player and regularly beat me with shots that ricocheted off the walls like cannonballs, but recently had been complaining of swollen wrists. Neither of us could foresee that in twenty years' time she would be crippled by rheumatoid arthritis.

On the Saturday, after double checking the tide tables the night beforehand, we tacked up the River Alde in her clinker-built boat and back again, skirting the treacherous mud banks and the pock-marked flats. On their outer reaches we could see the red and white stripes of the distinctive Orford lighthouse that warned passing ships of the dangers and guided them through the hazards. It looked like an outsized barber's pole.

The timbers of the boat's old hull creaked and groaned as the wind filled her sails, and the wooden decks shuddered in response. It was an exhilarating day. Across the water lay the mysterious and forbidden spit of shingle owned by the Ministry of Defence and reputed to have sinister Porton Down connections. During the Cold War it was the site of secret military testing. Members of the public were still banned. The stocky Martello tower built during the Napoleonic wars to foil French incursions squatted in the distance.

That evening we relaxed in front of the fire in her brick and flint cottage and ate a supper of freshly caught fish and warm local beer that smelled of hops. On the way up to bed I forgot to duck beneath a low-lying beam half way up the stairs, and bumped my head hard against its edge. The bruise on my scalp lingered for weeks. On the Sunday morning we joined the dog owners walking their scampering pets on Aldeburgh's steep shingle beach, forced off their customary lanes onto the exposed foreshore. The sharp wind made us hunch our shoulders and dig our hands deep inside our pockets before warming ourselves with thick slices of bread and ham bought from the nearby smoker

Back in London a forgotten leaflet in the bottom of my suitcase informed me that the Martello tower was built using 750,000 bricks. The walls are three meters thick.

In March 2001 I send a request in writing to the Library saying I wish to visit for research purposes. The reply from the Curator for Reader Services comes a week later. I learn that the Library is open by prior appointment only, with no access at weekends. He wants to know what dates I intend to be in Aldeburgh so that we can '…discuss in more detail the materials that you hope to study.' The helpful printed handouts accompanying his letter confirm that the Library was set up as a joint enterprise steered by Britten and Pears to provide a working resource that would also house their personal collections. There are the standard regulations with one surprising inclusion: I won't be allowed '…to eat, drink, smoke, or chew gum anywhere on the library premises.' The reference to gum has surely to be intended for the Library's visitors from the United States where Britten and Pears spent the war years between 1939 and 1942 before returning to England and successfully applying to become registered conscientious objectors.

I duly sign and return the *Conditions of Access to Special Resources in The Britten-Pears Library Collections,* and on a chilly Monday morning set off in my car for the small Suffolk coastal town that Benjamin Britten put on the map when it became home to the annual Aldeburgh Festival and The Britten-Pears Foundation. The route takes me through the much-maligned county of Essex and on to Suffolk, skirting Chelmsford, Colchester and Ipswich on the way

When I arrive at the Foundation I am pressed for further information about the nature of my research, so tell the librarian that I am specifically looking for any letters or coverage of the incidents when a woman claiming to be Britten's wife invaded *The Turn of the Screw* performances in 1955, and that I am considering a dramatic treatment. My reply is intentionally vague; I am wary of disclosing a personal agenda, afraid that it may compromise my access, that an admission of mere curiosity will make me appear unprofessional, not serious. A dramatic treatment sounds more credible. And it's true – I have already considered the possibilities for a story, even a film script. I am then shown to the reading room and left alone to go through files of old press cuttings and Festival catalogues while my request is looked into.

As expected, the programmes confirm *The Turn of the Screw* was put on three times during the Eighth Aldeburgh Festival, with Britten at the podium, on 18, 20 and 23 June, but curiously enough the cuttings file for that year is almost empty, unlike the crammed cuttings file for the '56 Festival. Given that *The Turn of the Screw* was billed as the signature event of the 1955 Festival repertoire, this has to be significant. The opera had received its premiere in Venice less than a year beforehand, so by any yardstick its inclusion in the Festival schedule under the baton of the composer would have been a notable event.

Instead it looks as if the file has been thoroughly eviscerated – in order, I cannot help speculating, to remove entirely any accounts of the woman's disastrous onstage interventions. Or maybe it was never reported in the press at all, but if so why is so much other coverage of the '55 Festival missing as well. Perhaps there's a clue in the Library's insistence that visitors may be asked to submit any bags on entering and leaving for 'inspection', a euphemism I suspect to foil light fingers. Or maybe I'm right, and there's another darker explanation altogether?

Meanwhile I start to get restless. Four hours later I am still waiting to hear if there is any documentation supporting the story so go off to get a sandwich for lunch.

When I get back I find the Library's director, a young woman called Dr Jenny Doctor, waiting for me. She asks why I am interested in the story, where I had discovered it, and what are my motives? I repeat that I am looking at using the event, as reported by Duncan in his Britten memoir, for a dramatic treatment. But why, she persists, why do I think this is of any interest? For me the answer is self-evident – a tale of love and unrequited passion for one of England's most famous composers against a dramatic Festival backdrop. What could be more compelling? She seems puzzled. Apparently I am the first person to have ever enquired about the event in question.

I then ask her whether Humphrey Carpenter, Britten's most recent biographer, had not also asked about this, but quickly realise I have unwittingly raised another sensitive, indeed inflammatory issue. Jenny Doctor reveals that the Foundation gave Carpenter almost unfettered access to their files, and the trustees are still bruised by what they regarded as his betrayal in writing at length, and often in graphic detail, about Britten's homosexuality and his penchant for post-pubescent boys. In their view this amounted to a terminal breach of the trust they had placed in Carpenter by allowing him privileged sight of the records, and they remain bitter.

Jenny Doctor adds that she has spent the morning ringing around the trustees to tell them of my request which, it appears, has caused ripples of consternation. For a moment I wonder if they fear I may be a relative of the woman, and that my explanations about research and a dramatic treatment are merely a cover story – that I may have a different, more sinister agenda altogether.

She then confirms that the incident did indeed take place, and produces a related letter from Britten to Ronald Duncan with a reference to a 'Miss T', the woman in question. I am given sight of the letter only, not a copy, but that's enough. At long last I have unequivocal confirmation that the Duncan account was based on fact, and that a Miss T was the woman concerned. A further revelation is still to come: the Foundation holds a wealth of correspondence between Britten and his lawyer, Isador Caplan, about the mysterious Miss T, but it was given to the Library by Caplan after his death under the terms of a sealed bequest, and the trustees are not minded to approve any breach of the strict confidentiality terms.

Jenny Doctor is unable to enlighten me any further on the content of the correspondence. Instead she suggests I write her a letter formally asking if the trustees will consider giving me access. Mindful that they will still be wary after the Carpenter experience I doubt this will achieve any result, but thank her for her help and walk back to the car park, shoulders clenched against the chill, wondering if I have come up against a wall of silence.

CHAPTER 5

Aldeburgh

The next morning I set out to explore the town more thoroughly on foot. I have my camera with me to take photographs of Crag House, Britten's home from 1949 to 1957 where he lived with Peter Pears, and of the Jubilee Hall a few doors down, wedged between Crag Path and Crabbe Street. An English Heritage blue plaque mounted on the front wall of Crag House identifies him simply as 'composer'. He was made a Freeman of Aldeburgh in 1962.

On the other side of the Path the town's shingle beach slopes down to the North Sea, a reminder of my previous visit. On fine days the gently ebbing waves lap its edges and families gather with their buckets and spades and picnics, their bathing suits and precautionary windbreaks. When the weather changes the sea turns a hostile grey and the breakers crash down, scattering the pebbles and driving visitors away apart from a few hardy all-weather enthusiasts. The lifeboat station opposite the hall is flanked by a row of assorted fishermen's huts and the town's war memorial juts up further along the beach in the opposite direction. The small fishing boats and a cluster of faded dinghies tethered against the low sea wall in the lee of the Path complete a classic seaside scene.

I am keen to see the sites of the festival events in person, sites that the teacher would have visited herself, and to try and gain some sense of the febrile atmosphere that she was sucked into, an atmosphere that appears to have eventually robbed her of her remaining sanity.

First on the list is a visit to the Hall. It backs virtually on to the seafront, a sturdy rectangular building made of red brick with bright blue double doors tucked inside a corner entrance porch on the side facing Crabbe Street. The stage door is discreetly located down a side passage towards the rear. Fortuitously it is already open for an Antiques and Collectors' Fair so I wander in and have a good look around. The interior is gloomily unremarkable apart from a high triple window that lets in much-needed sunlight, with rows of tiered seating below. It reminds me of the village halls of my childhood. Despite the modest activity, the shelves of second-hand books and the stalls with their bric-a-brac and craft wares, it still smells musty and unused. *The Turn of the Screw* would have been performed on the raised stage at the far end, the orchestra squeezed in front between the stage and the conductor's podium.

I try to imagine how it would have looked and felt when filled with people dressed for the occasion, to conjure up the excitement, the hum of conversation, the buzz of anticipation, and the sounds of the musicians tuning their violins before the sudden hush as Britten entered and strode to assume his place, baton in hand.

But the village hall atmosphere is hard to expunge. Distracting memories from my childhood return, memories of vegetable competitions at A&P shows, giant leeks, onions and pumpkins vying for the coveted red rosettes, and in the pens outside immaculately groomed sheep and cattle waiting to be judged while children on ponies trotted around the show ring and adult riders jumped over brushwood fences and triple bars.

I remind myself that I am standing in the place where it all happened, that this is the place where the stage was invaded by the woman claiming to be his wife.

In a moment of epiphany, I realise how truly awful it must have been, not just for Britten, the cast, and the members of the orchestra, but for the audience too. The hall still feels small in spite of having been recently extended, and its restricted size at the time would have grossly amplified the impact of her agony. This intimate encounter with such a searing event must have been profoundly shocking. But when I ask my landlady about it later that evening her friendliness evaporates as her face closes up like a clam, and I see that I have crossed a line.

Nonetheless I am on a quest, I remind myself, and there is more to see. Back outside I take a deep breath of the sea air and marshal my resolve. Next on the list are the churches, St Peter's and St Paul's – the parish church on Victoria Road, the Library and the Baptist church on the High Street, opposite the Festival office. The Roman Catholic church is at the other end of Church Walk.

In my hand is a copy I've managed to find of the 1955 Festival programme listing the events and venues:

1955 Festival Programme Eighth Festival

18–26 June 1955: Operatic
18, 20 and 23 June 1955: Britten, The Turn of the Screw, conducted by the composer.

Other
18 June 1955: Amadeus String Quartet (Parish Church)
19 June 1955: Recital/Peter Pears and Benjamin Britten (Jubilee Hall)
20 June 1955: Recital (JH)
21 June 1955: Orchestral Concert/Walter Goehr (PC)

22 June 1955: Brain Wind Quintet (PC)
24 June 1955: Purcell Singers (PC), Recital/Frederick Fuller and Julian Bream (JH)
25 June 1955: Choral and Orchestral Concert (PC)
26 June 1955: Music on the Meare/Aldeburgh Music Club (Thorpeness), Opera Concert (JH)

I note that it covers musical performances only. Other venues in and around Aldeburgh were roped in for the various ancillary events that added to the Festival offer, the lectures, exhibitions, film screenings, and the opening wine festival.

I visit the different sites in turn, guided by Duncan. In the Festival calendar Aldeburgh remained the dominant venue until the conversion and completion of the concert hall at the Snape Maltings centre in 1967. Back in 1955 the Church Hall on Victoria Road was the preferred site for the principal art exhibitions, with the cinema on the High Street screening suitable art-house films. Elsewhere lectures by various experts were delivered in the Union Baptist Chapel, while the brass bands continued to commandeer their traditional position on The Green by the town's 16th century Moot Hall.

But despite my best efforts the out-of-season atmosphere is pervasive, and curiously dispiriting. The sight of Britten's grave in the parish churchyard's lawn cemetery, with Peter Pears' simple matching headstone beside it, does little to dispel my mood. The headstones are plain to a fault, devoid of the Dearly Beloved inscriptions on their neighbours. Peeling cigarette butts disfigure the sad tufts of grass struggling around their bases. A pair of crows caw hoarsely from their perch on the branches of a nearby tree, and for all its glowing colours, John Piper's Britten memorial window inside the church fails to lift the prevailing gloom of the sullen day. The town feels atrophied as it waits for the winter to end, for the days to lengthen, and for the coming spring to restore it to life.

I had eaten a solitary supper of fish and chips in a High Street restaurant the night before, seated on my own at a cream formica table, its surface scarred with cigarette burns, feeling like a stranger. I realise that if I am to establish any connection with Aldeburgh it will have to be through the eyes of the woman who believed she was Britten's wife.

CHAPTER 6

Wall of Silence

The following week I post off the letter to Jenny Doctor for forwarding to the trustees. I have thought long and hard about how to phrase my request:

> *Further to our meeting on 26 March I am writing to confirm that I would welcome the opportunity to find out more about the incident referred to in the Ronald Duncan memoir, and recall that you mentioned both Dr Donald Mitchell and Marion Thorpe may be able to offer a first hand account.*
>
> *I am particularly keen to establish the facts as far as possible in the absence of any other published references given my interest in exploring the potential of this episode for a dramatic treatment. If either Trustee would agree to meet me I'd be enormously grateful.*
>
> *Obviously the Duncan account – brief as it is – already offers a peg for an imaginative treatment, but I appreciate there are real sensitivities about the episode and am keen to approach the subject as responsibly as possible, hence my visit already to the Britten-Pears Library.*

> *In the same spirit it would be most helpful if the Trustees could exceptionally offer me access to the documents you referred to. I would, of course, undertake to treat any such documents in the strictest confidence with the intention that access should assist a fully informed approach rather than provide material for use.*

The letter drops into the red pillar box at the end of my street with a soft thud. Timid, courteous, respectful. Another step as my search for yet more facts inches forward.

Meanwhile I have finished the Humphrey Carpenter biography, *Benjamin Britten: A Biography,* published in 1992. It is a comprehensive account, and highly readable. But I can see why the Foundation's trustees were so affronted. Carpenter dwells at length on Britten's relationship with young boys and the callous way he discarded them once they became adolescents.

Some were local boys from humble backgrounds he notes, boys who felt such rejection all the more keenly, cast adrift from hopes for the richer, more glamorous life that Britten's attentions had introduced them to so tantalizingly. In Carpenter's account the nights at Crag House, evenings when Britten sat watching them have a bath, holding large warm towels at the ready for when they climbed out of the cooling water, clean and scrubbed, become distant memories. Prospects are abandoned, lost to the onset of physical maturity, breaking voices, and the whims of a man who replaces them one after the other with younger versions.

Carpenter also writes in arguably questionable taste about the nature of the sexual relationship between Britten and Pears, and is unsparing when exposing Pears' promiscuity. But oddly enough there is not a hint of the event involving the woman that Duncan mentioned. I'm at a loss to understand why. Carpenter seems to have had a well-developed nose for gossip and intrigue, and this surely would have been worthy of inclusion, so I decide it's time to send him a letter asking if he knew about the incident in question, and if so why he failed to mention it, especially in view of the distress Duncan said it caused to Britten in his own account.

The letter is dated 20 April 2001:

Dear Mr Carpenter,

I read your biography of Benjamin Britten recently with interest and enjoyment. Since then I have been involved in a research project of my own, prompted in part by the mention in the Ronald Duncan memoir of a woman who, in the mid-1950s, became obsessed by Benjamin Britten to the point where she believed she was his wife and who disrupted the opening performance of The Turn of the Screw.

I have approached the Britten-Pears Library about the incident, seeking further information, but apart from confirming that the library holds a body of correspondence between Benjamin Britten and his lawyer about the episode, they have been unable to help me. The correspondence is not available for examination.

In view of their acknowledgement of this episode and the Duncan memoir, I was wondering if you would be able to throw any further light on the matter. Whilst I appreciate that you did not mention it in your Britten biography, I would be most grateful if your researches were able to expand on the Duncan account.

I am surprised to get a telephone call from Carpenter a few days later. I had been expecting him to get back to me in writing, and am caught off guard. He sounds prickly, defensive, and I get the distinct impression that he regrets he didn't include the incident, or worse, overlooked it altogether. He blusters that he thought the Ronald Duncan autobiography was unreliable before offering to intercede with the Foundation on my behalf to help me gain access to the bequest. I don't have the heart, or nerve, to tell him that this would be unhelpful given the Foundation's views of him.

In the interim I still haven't heard back from Jenny Doctor, so send her another email, asking whether she has been able to take any soundings yet as to whether Dr Donald Mitchell or Marion Thorpe are prepared to meet with me, or grant me access to the Britten/Caplan archive.

In truth my request is a disingenuous tactic, offered primarily for form's sake. Whilst access to the files would undoubtedly satisfy my curiosity, if they disclose no connection at all between my teacher and 'Miss T', my theory evaporates. On the other hand, if the files do disclose a connection I'm already compromised by my written assurances that I will respect confidentiality terms. In any case I am certain that the deeply protective trustees will not be forthcoming, and so it proves. The following day Jenny Doctor sends me their response.

> *After very careful consideration, the Trustees have asked me to inform you that they will not make an exception to their policy concerning public access to legal files: the legal files dealing with the woman who claimed to be married to Britten will not be opened. As I explained when you were here the legal files here have never been opened to researchers for reason of confidentiality.*
>
> *I've also been asked to relay to you that neither Dr Mitchell nor Mrs Thorpe are available to discuss the issue with you. In point of fact, neither was personally involved with the situation when it happened, and they do not feel that exploring the subject now would contribute to anyone's understanding of Britten. Having had a chance to think about it much more than when we spoke, I don't believe that any of Britten's associates who were actually*

involved with the situation is (sic) still alive.

I know that you will be disappointed by these decisions, but I can assure you that your requests were carefully considered.

So that's it. My dilemma is resolved. I have to accept that the trustees have acted in accordance with the terms of the bequest, and I appreciate Jenny Doctor's efforts on my behalf. But I'm also acutely aware that I lack agency; I am not an academic, nor an established writer, and I chose not to disclose my own belief that the woman could have been my former teacher. Perhaps I should have been more transparent too.

I subsequently learn from a retired member of the orchestra for *The Turn of the Screw*, corroborated by another, second source, that they too were physically present when the first incident took place, and that Britten was immensely distressed. But like the trustees they also refuse to meet me, leaving me with the unmistakable impression that the people of Aldeburgh remain invincibly loyal to their most famous resident and share an unspoken view that this painful incident should be erased from the town's collective memory. Erased, buried and forgotten.

I am sympathetic but undeterred, especially since the wealth of unseen correspondence between Britten and Caplan, the body of legal files, continues to suggest more complex issues that feed into my heightened imagination, issues involving confidentiality, the need to suppress possibly damaging facts, or developments touching on possible litigation? And if so on what grounds? Why the secrecy? Would disclosure open the way to legal challenges, claims for compensation? Or allegations of coercion? Questions, questions.

Crucially however, I now have sufficient information from the Foundation and my other sources to go ahead with the story I've been nursing for so long, a story about great love and frustrated passion, based on one woman's tragic obsession with a man who was a musical genius and a known homosexual at a time when overt homosexuality was still a crime. The woman surely knew this at some level, but deniability is the root of delusion. When it becomes pathological it enters the realms of tragedy.

Still missing is the key that will connect the mysterious Miss T to my own Miss Verne, assuming that was ever her real name, but my gut instincts are undiminished and I remain convinced, now more than ever, that the two women were one and the same. Time to create a fictional version of the teacher's history and her state of mind, and to construct my own version of the path her infatuation took instead, to create answers when there are none. I am unable to do this on my own. She must become my accomplice in the telling of this story.

After all, other writers have blurred the line between fiction and reality with impunity when it serves their purpose, so I will follow their example and do the same. Above all this is my story, both through personal experience, and by default. I own the narrative, and therefore its treatment is my decision alone. It is a liberating moment. As Mark Twain said, 'Never let the truth get in the way of a good story.' From now on this will be my credo.

But where to start? I need to find out more about what shaped the woman's state of mind and fed her fantastical notions, and discover the term erotomanic disorder, first identified in 1921 by the French psychiatrist, Gaëtan Gatian de Clérambault, as a delusional sub-type associated with stalking.

In 1997 stalking became a criminal offence in the United Kingdom under terms outlined in the Protection from Harassment Act (PHA), with sanctions including fines and, in extreme cases, imprisonment. The act continues to struggle with definitions and behaviours, and is constantly being revised to cover newer aspects such as cyberstalking. Over the years increasing attention has been given to impacts on victims who are supported by a national stalking helpline.

More recent research has revealed that close on 40 per cent of UK members of parliament have experienced stalking behaviour from their constituents, and newspapers and other media regularly carry distressing accounts where outcomes have proved calamitous. John Hinckley's attempt to assassinate ex-President Ronald Reagan, for example, was motivated it is alleged by a morbid attempt to gain actress Jodie Foster's attention.

It wasn't until 2002, however, that psychologists came up with a more topical term that appears a perfect fit – Celebrity Worship, essentially an extreme extension of obsessed fan behaviour. It is commonly associated with stalking which, according to psychologists specialising in this area, has three classic presentations: Simple Obsessional, Love Obsessional, and Erotomanic, where the stalker believes the object, usually referred to as the victim, returns their love.

The first presentation, Simple Obsessional, is usually found in men who have already had a previous relationship with their victim. Love Obsessional, stage two of the syndrome, is more often found in people suffering from paranoia or schizophrenia.

However it is the relatively rare erotomanic presentation that I am most interested in, and which appears to offer the most relevant diagnosis. It affects women in the main and indeed, at one time was referred to as Old Maid's Insanity before the more progressive designation became accepted parlance.

Apparently erotomanic stalkers genuinely believe their love is reciprocated, and in nearly every case their victim, usually from a higher social bracket, is already famous and therefore unattainable. Historic targets include John Maynard Keynes who became one such 'object' in the early 1900s. Another characteristic is their persistent denial of inconvenient facts, like marriage, or in this case, Britten's homosexuality.

Such stalkers also tend to believe they share a secret language with their victims, and that the love object is communicating with them via special signals or a shared private code. They are loners, often suffering from fragile self-esteem and a range of related psychiatric disorders including schizophrenia at the more extreme margins. Fantasies about intimate meetings in private are not uncommon, likewise sending letters or unwelcome gifts, and visiting a victim's home unannounced. The condition can last for weeks, months, or in some cases indefinitely. If the condition is what is termed 'fixed', successful treatment outcomes are unlikely.

The Celebrity Worship syndrome provides an explanation that frames and contextualises her behaviour at last. She even matches the personality profile – a socially awkward, isolated loner with a history of depression, detached from her family, sexually inexperienced. I have found the route into her past that I was seeking.

CHAPTER 7

In the Beginning

I now enter a different realm, one where I need to construct a childhood that offers a credible background for this mystery woman who came seemingly from nowhere, and then abruptly disappeared. Actual events and timelines must be blended with invention or assumptions to bridge the narrative gaps. As a colonial living in England, and therefore an outlier, I will start by drawing upon the observations I have made over the years of the English, and the ways in which family units are often morbidly compressed into the space of a single household, with cousins who have never met each other, and uncles and aunts who are strangers.

Coming as I do from a large household myself, with an extended family of relatives running literally into the hundreds, and from a part of the country where it sometimes feels as if everyone of my generation is connected through marriage or consanguinity and the shared colonial experience, this is an arid aspect I had not anticipated prior to my arrival at the port of Tilbury back in the mid-60s. England can be a lonely place for many of its own I discovered, the lives of its inhabitants bounded by suburbs, urban drift, regional accents, social barriers, rigid class distinctions, and possibly lingering wartime dislocations and historic traumatic bereavements that I will always struggle to comprehend.

Based on my impressions, I decide to place her in an unexceptional middle-class household vaguely located in a small town in England's north-west – Huddersfield, going by the postcards, the youngest by some years of three children, her parents' autumn leaf. I have a sense that this is the kind of inherently dysfunctional background I need to deploy, with its institutional hinterland of suppression and hidden psychosis. Her father, let's say, is a partner with a local accountancy firm. The mother reflects the times in her role as a conventional housewife who also happens to have a modest talent as a pianist, but whose gift has been subverted by domesticity.

The war comes and goes, but the worst of its effects bypass the family. Their village is well off the routes taken by enemy aircraft, and her father has been exempted from military service on account of his age. Instead he enlists in the local home guard and plays his part in requisitioning vehicles, monitoring petrol usage and winkling out any putative fifth columnists who may be lurking treacherously in the community.

Her mother joins the Women's Institute and welcomes the camaraderie she shares with the other women. She has always been a person of limited ambition, and the socks and gloves she knits for the boys at the front satisfy the requirement to make a contribution, however modest, to the country's war effort. She is doubly relieved that her responsibilities to her growing family shield her from more onerous demands, like working in a munitions factory, or driving a tractor. The very thought makes her check her carefully filed fingernails for reassurance.

Her parents are vaguely concerned that their youngest child seems to have no friends. No other girls come around to play, and invitations to birthday parties are few and far between, usually driven by her mother's friendships instead, so when the girl turns ten they decide it is time for her to follow in her mother's footsteps and learn the piano too. A safe, conventional choice. Besides, the old upright in the lounge needs to be played more to justify the space it occupies, and because it is a solo instrument rather than an orchestral one they judge it will better suit their daughter's faltering temperament. The individual attention of a good, even adequate piano teacher will, they hope, help build her confidence and develop any latent abilities. The decision appears to have been the right one. She has inherited her mother's keyboard skills, and the hours of solitary practice suit her introverted nature. From the local primary school she progresses to a nearby girls' secondary school, scraping through the entry exam, and continues her weekly piano lessons. But the transition into the teenage years is a fraught time and the mirror in her bedroom becomes her enemy. She is repelled by the changes in her body and is soon forcing her fingers down her throat, vomiting up the meals she has just eaten in a futile effort to cling on to her vanishing childhood, to impose some semblance of control over what is happening to her.

It is all done in secret, and perhaps this is where she establishes control most of all. Her parents either don't know what is happening, or choose to ignore it in a very English excess of denial. Her sister probably guesses, but colludes with the unspoken agreement in the family that any aberrant behavior will right itself in time.

The age gap tells, compounded by an unspoken acknowledgment that disclosure will serve no purpose other than engender embarrassment. At the time mental illness is treated by families as a shameful secret, tantamount to having a child born with birth defects, but a problem that will right itself in due course if ignored as far as possible. The term, bulimia, has yet to find its way into the lexicon of post-pubescent angst. A propensity for secrecy and a tendency towards self-absorption become embedded precursors of her future mental health.

Meanwhile, with each birthday the old piano becomes more and more a refuge where she can escape from the adolescent doubts and uncertainties that disrupt her days and nights, and focus instead on the discipline of scales, of rippling arpeggios, and learn to listen, to truly listen. As she gets older the wrenching, mood-changing shifts from major to minor keys make her heart lurch and her ears ring. She watches her fingers ripple along the keyboard and back again in tandem, and searches out cadences and chords in an excess of sometimes dizzying exploration. Czerny becomes her technical mentor and accomplice, and chromatic scales a pathway to feelings she cannot explain.

But for some reason the same sense of exhilaration is missing when she plays the conventional repertoire of eighteenth and nineteenth century composers so favoured in the nation's classrooms. The crotchets, quavers, the broad open minims and the jumbled semiquavers with their busy connecting tails cluttering the scores impose inviolable, non-negotiable strictures. The harmonies sound too predictable, too familiar, and the melodies too accessible. When she makes mistakes the dissonances are often more surprising, more exciting, and the resolutions more satisfying. The emergent sense of exploration becomes a purpose in itself.

So it is not surprising that she starts developing a preference for the twentieth century composers instead, and encouraged by one of her teachers she is soon borrowing recordings from the town's lending library, recordings of works by the great Russians like Shostakovitch and Rachmaninov, Mahler, the English school – Delius, Elgar, and one of the newest and most exciting of them all, Benjamin Britten, who started writing his first compositions when he was only five and is already called a genius.

She discovers him while her tastes are still forming. The same teacher introduces her to his chamber music and nurtures her newfound enthusiasm. She is younger than the other teachers, and in consequence less attached to the traditional repertoires of older pedagogues. Under her guidance the girl studies music theory to better understand the calibrated discords and transitions, the leaping intervals and soaring top lines. The pieces she learns to play, piano adaptations of works like *The Young Apollo, Les Illuminations, Twelve Variations,* appeal to her developing ear, and his modernism feels like strangely familiar territory that excites her already heightened senses. Her unalloyed pleasure in his canticles makes the conversion complete.

Her schooldays end with limited academic success, the piano aside. Her parents, pragmatists both, encourage her to get a teaching diploma, pointing out that this will ensure she can get jobs teaching music wherever she wishes. They are looking forward to time on their own, free from parental responsibilities. At the teacher's training college her tutor guides her through Britten's output as she shapes her dissertation and explores his relationship with contemporary theorists and composers like Berg and Field. When she takes up her first post at a school for girls shortly after the war has ended she embraces opportunities to hear his works in the great English concert venues, often travelling hundreds of miles by train to hear thrilling, live performances. The imposing entrance to Huddersfield's train station becomes a familiar part of her landscape. The words of his song cycles, his canticles, and above all his operas – *Peter Grimes, The Rape of Lucretia, Billy Budd, Albert Herring, Gloriana,* all prompt a growing appetite for textual scrutiny and analysis. Librettos acquire new meanings that she examines minutely, going over them again and again. The more she reads the greater the sense of some profound connection. At some point she attaches a personal relevance to them. They speak of her, and to her. From there it is only a short step before she ascribes the relevance to herself. She becomes convinced she has found a mind that she can identify with, that this man is her soul mate.

Her parents help her buy a small flat on the outskirts of the town with just enough room for the piano. They are relieved when she finally leaves home, and doubly relieved when she promptly finds a teaching post. In the evenings and at weekends she continues to listen to the recordings she has bought of his works or borrowed from the library, playing them over and over again until she knows them by heart. In between she spends hours at the keyboard, exploring tones and nuances, memorizing every note.

Sometimes she sings the words as well in her thin contralto, becoming her own accompanist. A Grove's dictionary sits on her bookshelf alongside the musical scores and libretti she has accumulated over the years. *The Serenade*, the *Donne Sonnets*, the words that accompany Lucretia's entrance: 'Whenever we are made to part we live within each other's heart, both waiting, each wanting.'[7] They all speak to her directly, consolidating the growing sense of her own uniqueness. Because she has never developed a gift for friendship she feels no need for friends. Her time is already fully absorbed and satisfied by her escalating passion. Her interior life becomes her dominant life, feeding into a latent romanticism that thrives on her self-imposed isolation

And once a week she pores over her latest copy of *The Radio Times*, marking with her pen any broadcast slots featuring performances of his works or relevant talks. The pages of her accompanying journals soon fill with quotations taken from his librettos and notes about the broadcasts she has listened to, how they have affected her, what she has thought of the performances. The entries mount up, a record that she can return to whenever the doubts assail her, a record of conversations with herself, a source of comfort and ownership. In another box she keeps the newspaper articles she assiduously collects, carefully cut and annotated, pasted onto plain backing sheets of A4 and filed in date order with an unremitting attention to detail. The detail is important because it is another area where she can exercise the control she needs in a life without any practical emotional core.

On the few occasions she goes out with male colleagues or the occasional fellow concertgoer who has approached her during an interval, the conversations in cafes, or across restaurant tables, are stilted and directionless. She has never developed a gift for small talk, and her reticence and reserve are formidable barriers to the easy intimacy of friendship. Eventually the other women teachers give up, defeated by her refusal to engage with their overtures, deciding she's 'odd'. For a while there is a young man from Bethesda in Wales, a music teacher like her, with Celtic colouring and a lilting Welsh accent, who asks her out repeatedly and urges her to join the choir he sings in. Challenged by her inscrutability and defensiveness, he persists until he acknowledges defeat, tired of paying for meals and buying flowers without any tangible return. The intensity of her regard for Britten, a constant unseen presence, is an immovable impediment.

All too soon she finds herself wondering which concert will be the most fitting way to mark her thirtieth birthday. She is still single, still teaching, but her complexion has started to lose the bloom of youth and her clothes are becoming dowdy. When she first started teaching it was often fun, satisfying, offering pleasure and rewards when a girl showed talent, but after ten years in a succession of different schools she is obliged to accept the harsh truth that she is an adequate teacher at best, unable to establish that vital connection that will bring out the spark in a promising pupil. The hours are now compressed into little more than a way of negotiating the weekdays, punctuated by the old bouts of depression that return periodically, bouts when she is forced to question anew who she is, and ask where her life is leading. She feels her life unraveling, going into reverse, that she has no future beyond a diminishing present, and the depression returns.

The brother and sister are married, but her increasing self-absorption does not allow for an interest in them either, or the lives of their young children, her nieces and nephews. The disinterest is mutual, underpinned by the age differences. Her connection with her family becomes reduced to a few key events, like significant birthdays and Christmases.

The one constant is the composer. As her teaching duties become more and more onerous, so she becomes more and more dependent on his work, on the recordings and concerts, and her admiration becomes more and more insistent. The vacuum at the centre of her own life makes her perilously vulnerable to the dreams that start to consume her. What started off as the simple admiration of a fan morphs incrementally into a syndrome verging on the obsessive.

She has recognized the messages encoded in his music and captured in the lyrics, lyrics like the beautiful lines in his *Wedding Anthem:* messages intended for her:

> These two are not two
> Love has made them one
> Amo Ergo Sum!
> And by its mystery
> Each is no less but more
> Amo Ergo Sum
> For to love is to be
> And in loving Him, I love Thee!
> Amo Ergo Sum[8]

Meanwhile she continues to take every opportunity to watch the composer in concert hall after concert hall, her savings poured into a pilgrimage of affirmation as she follows his concert schedules avidly, buying tickets whenever possible for the duets and the solo recitals when he sits at the piano imbued with authority, his body erect in immaculate evening dress. If she chooses her seat carefully she is able to watch his hands and study his technique, the way his hands flow up and down the keyboard, wrists level, the fingers held like bells, and wait for the extension of the notes and the chords that close a passage when he raises his arms in conclusion, leaving the sounds shimmering in the air. The reflections of his fingers in the gleaming black lids of the concert grands, the Steinways and the Bechsteins, mirror his facility as he commands the keyboard with a consummate skill.

Urged on by her admiration she decides to send him a postcard of Beata Beatrix, Lizzie Siddal, muse to Dante Gabriel Rossetti. The resonance is compelling and her message a simple one. 'I am an admirer of yours,' she writes, 'especially the way you blend lyrics and music to create such profound messages. Yours, J.'

She seals it inside an envelope – the message is for his eyes only, and writes the address. She has done her research: Crag House, 4 Crabbe Street, Aldeburgh, Suffolk. It feels like reaching out through the cosmos, responding to a summons. He has been on his own quest for a soul mate. His messages have found their intended recipient at last.

Over the next few months the cards will become steadily more explicit, and then be replaced by the letters.

When the first card arrives he isn't surprised. He receives many from his admirers, but soon these ones are dropping into his postbox with increasing frequency and the scrawled messages are becoming disturbingly intimate, claiming a connection that doesn't exist, referring to messages he has never sent. He sets them aside, all twelve of them, just in case.

CHAPTER 8

Venice

In 1954 she makes a bold decision and fills in a passport application. She has decided to go to Venice with an opera lovers' group to see the premiere that September of his newest opera, *The Turn of the Screw,* at the city's Teatro La Fenice. The storyline is based on the short horror story of the same title by Henry James, and she reads it conscientiously by way of preparation. Over five days she will be in the at times claustrophobic company of eleven other Britten admirers.

It is her first time in Italy. Her first time abroad in fact. She buys a guidebook and learns some Italian phrases in advance, aware that her musical vocabulary of *diminuendo, andante, largo, fortissimo,* is unlikely to meet her needs. She practises how to say thank you, *grazie,* and goodbye, *arrivederci,* but the rolled 'r's are beyond her, and she rightly anticipates limited opportunities for *pizzicato.* She is also nervous about the food. Pasta and pizza have yet to find a place in the English cuisine. Olive oil is used for ear infections. Italian restaurants are associated with red and white checked tablecloths spotted with tomato sauce and wine stains, and empty chianti bottles in straw baskets, their necks plugged with candle stubs and their sides clogged with ancient deposits of melted wax. She hopes there will be options, preferably English ones. Any possible enthusiasm for a culinary adventure poses a step too far.

As the train chugs across the causeway linking the mainland to the city she looks out the carriage window, relieved that the long journey is coming to an end, transfixed as the city emerges into view through the haze while the mainland diminishes into the distance and the factory chimneys belching smoke recede into irrelevance. The sense of familiarity is entrancing, and astonishing. After the bomb-ravaged towns of England with their blistering craters filled with weeds and rubble, it is like going back in time to a pristine era embellished by its own beauty, redolent of continuity and permanence. She shares every visitor's wonderment and delight in this living museum and her spirits lift. She is relieved she doesn't have to make her way to the hotel on her own while her senses are being so assailed.

The impression of the city's self assurance and entitlement persists, part of its legacy and founded on a history that she now physically experiences for the first time. At the station the tour leader shepherds the group onto a water taxi that takes them along the Grand Canal to the vaporetto stop where they disembark and make their way to the hotel's campo. She feels she has been here forever. Every scene, every palazzo, every calle is already familiar, faithfully rendered in the Guardis and Canalettos she has seen hanging in London's National Gallery. The black gondolas with their gilded decoration and prows like condors look as they did hundreds of years ago. Only the gondoliers' clothing has changed. But while the beribboned straw hats and striped tops may be contemporary, their skills remain the same, passed on down through generations of the same families. The huge bronze horses cresting St Mark's bear daily witness to La Serenissima's rich mercantile and incursionary past, and the Doge's Palace sits like a magnificent confection behind its pink and white brickwork façade, ice cream and nougat, perched on twin rows of arched marble columns.

The next morning, rather than join the group tour she boldly decides to strike out and see the city on her own, guidebook in hand, ignoring the tour leader's pursed disapproval. But her map bears little relationship to reality and she is soon lost in the maze of canals and bridges, and the unexpected squares with their cafes and lavishly decorated churches.

The interiors smell of damp and incense and the walls are alive with scenes of saints writhing in agony or ecstasy. Shafts of celestial light pierce painted clouds, plump cherubs with dimpled thighs and buttocks float in the air light as gossamer, and thin votive tapers flicker in metal racks. She buys one and lights it, mouthing a prayer that says nothing, but a gesture nonetheless.

Above a sumptuous altar framed by twisted marble columns, Christ ascends in glory, a vision in swirling scarlet, arms upraised, floating heavenwards through a riot of angels with improbable wings sprouting from their shoulder blades. In a side chapel a withered foot the colour of parchment, with mummified toes, rests on a moth-eaten velvet cushion in a glass case and a black-clad priest emerges silently from behind a pillar and touches her bottom. She jumps aside awkwardly, wondering if this is normal in Venice or a figment of her imagination, and departs in a hurry, anxious suddenly to leave the gloom behind her, to escape back into the reassuring daylight and the fresh open air.

It is the year of the 27th Venice Biennale, the international contemporary art festival, and although its peak is over the city remains clogged with late-season art lovers. In the shop windows she is distracted by swirling marbled papers, leather-bound books, brilliant artists' pigments – red, alizarin, viridian, cobalt blue, saffron yellow, before making her way across the crowded Rialto Bridge and on to the market. Trays of octopus and squid compete with langoustines, grouper and sea bass; tomatoes of every shape and colour, red, green, yellow and purple, are piled high. After the limited range of produce in most English towns where the last vestiges of wartime rationing were only lifted a few months ago, the range of seafood, of fruit and vegetables, is almost overwhelming.

She pauses in front of another shop, arrested by the sight of a smiling horse's head painted on the window. Inside metal trays display hunks of glistening red flesh, a deeper, richer colour than the usual beef or lamb cuts in butchers' shops back home. Of course – cavallo. It's in the guidebook. She imagines the one-time owners of the bloody steaks she's looking at galloping across green fields and feasting on oats until they become too old to ride. Or broken down like Black Beauty's friend Ginger. Next door another shop sells salamis, some of them she is sure also made with horsemeat, and cheeses she has never seen before, their exposed interiors stippled with blue like varicose veins. Other shops sell sinister faceless masks with extended noses like beaks and blind slits for eyes. Hanging beside them are traditional black *tricornes*, edged with golden braid, waiting to be taken home as souvenirs.

From her vantage points on delicately arched bridges that all look confusingly similar she is distracted by the glowing red and gold tints of creepers and vines hanging down over the canals against cracked and crumbling walls and peeling stucco, a reminder that winter is around the corner. How strange that so much colour can be a harbinger of such a bereft season when the city's palette is reduced to a bleak grey, and fog and rain pervade the days in dismal repetition.

Her sense of location is only fully restored when she finds herself back in St Mark's Square, looking at the Doge's Palace as she sips an outdoors cup of ludicrously expensive coffee and wonders how to pay. The waiters gliding between the tables, immaculate in black and white, all look the same. Pigeons strut nearby, beady orange eyes alert for scraps. One flaps onto her table, its left foot an amputated stump. Groups of tourists cluster at the foot of the campanile, waiting for their own bird's eye view of the city before exploring the basilica's gloomy interior and golden tesserae. The clock tower strikes two. Down a small street behind the church she buys a slice of pizza for a late lunch. She will forever after link the city with Ben – her Ben. If it weren't for him she would never have come here. If it hadn't been for his summons she would not be experiencing such beauty mixed with such darkness and drama. This is what he wished for her. This is his gift.

She is less sure when it comes to her fellow travellers however, relieved she insisted on the extra expense of a single room rather than share with a stranger. Most of them are couples in any case. Several seem to know each other from previous tours to other opera venues, like Ravenna, Cork, New York. One or two appear to be musicians in their own right, others are self-proclaimed devotees of the Wigmore Hall, Opera House subscribers, members of amateur chamber groups. The competitive atmosphere and conversations are unsettling, corrosive. They soon separate into de facto cabals from which she is excluded, a single woman on her own, indeterminate, invisible. But why would she want to listen to the virtues of Torcello versus Murano, or the shrill displays of self-regarding knowledge? She isn't here for Harry's Bar and bellinis, nor for the Guggenheim or the Accademia. She's not like them, she's here for the opera, here for Ben.

More problematic is the shared conviction they exude, a conviction that they know Britten and his works intimately, and that their knowledge gives them privileged access to the man himself. In the face of so much dinner table certitude she has moments when she begins to doubt her relationship to him, to question again whether it is as unique as she thinks. Does he have space in his life for her after all, or is she a delusional fool? But no, the very thought is anathema. He deserves her trust, and her love. He has reached out to her, and she is duty bound to respond. It is a feeling that will follow her back to England, fuelling her obsession as she struggles with the precarious self-esteem that threatens daily to undermine her faith in the messages she continues to seek out by way of reassurance.

On the evening of the performance she dresses with the utmost care. He will be conducting his opera's premiere in one of the most famous opera houses in the world. She has read that women dress primarily for themselves, or for other women, but she is dressing for him only. How else to answer his calls, to honour his messages, 'So I my best beloved's am.' As she dabs scent behind her ears and applies a final dash of lipstick in front of the mirror, she replays the line over and over before wrapping herself in the blue velvet coat she has bought especially for the occasion. The colour suits her and she knows she's never looked better. Her cheeks are aglow with anticipation and her eyes sparkle. She smiles at her reflection once more, lifting her chin, tilting her face to one side, then picks up her evening bag and goes down to join the rest of the party in the hotel foyer.

The tour leader gives them a quick briefing before they leave. The opera was commissioned by the Biennale committee which accounts for its premiere at La Fenice before the traditional opera season opens in December. But he's told us all this already, she thinks, a man who's in love the sound of his own voice, who once he's started cannot stop. On and on he goes about how the event has been eagerly awaited in the opera world, a sure sign of the recognition Benjamin Britten, an English composer, a foreigner no less, commands in the home of opera, the land of Puccini and perhaps the greatest of them all, Verdi himself. When he pauses for breath everyone heads to the door in unison. They are of one mind and keen to get on their way.

It is only short walk from the hotel to the theatre. The party threads its way down a shadowed calle, then over another arched bridge at the same time as a gondolier glides his vessel beneath it, handling the long oar as gracefully as a ballet dancer. In the dying golden sunlight of the early evening the narrow canals and the reflections of the buildings, the faded hues of cream, burnt umber, pinks, blues, russet reds, have never looked more beautiful. Then there it is, the modest façade with its neo-classical Palladio-style columns flanking the entrance from the campo that has abruptly opened up in front of them.

For a moment she is disappointed, let down even. The building looks too small, too constricted for its reputation. The frontage is too narrow. But the first impression is misleading. In the crowded foyer men and women in evening dress are greeting each other in a melee of different languages – German, English, French, Italian, others she doesn't recognize, and the interior with its five tiers of boxes glitters like a fairytale birthday cake dipped in diamonds. She is transfixed by the gilded swirls of decoration festooning every surface, the great chandelier hanging from the painted ceiling that sparkles back in the mirrors, and the bare-breasted phoenixes leaning forward from the heights like bowsprits. But unlike Covent Garden, this theatre is also altogether more intimate, more quintessentially Italian. The muted green walls at the back of the boxes speak of discretion, not braggadocio.

There is also a palpable tension beneath the excitement, anxious glances. She overhears whispers in corners. Britten had to finish the work with his left hand because of a painful attack of bursitis, his assistants had to do some last-minute physical notation for him instead, the stage crew have threatened to go on strike, putting the live broadcast in doubt. But at the last minute the disputes are resolved and everything goes according to plan. The opera's darkness, the ghosts that populate its cast, echo the mood of night-time Venice where every alleyway becomes a trap and every canal a prelude to drowning, and as the singers' voices rise and fall she finds herself thinking of all the corpses that have floated beneath the city's bridges over the centuries, of the skeletons mired in decades of mud and sludge, weighed down by the stones and rocks that tether them to their graves, resistant still to the ebb and pull of the tides and autumn floods.

For all that they are dead, the ghosts of Quint and Miss Jessel have never felt more real with their undercurrents of depravity and abuse. The face of Quint is the face of Peter Pears in the tenor role; the boy soprano playing Miles follows slyly in his footsteps, the embodiment of corrupted innocence. In 1956 the same boy's voice breaks during a Paris performance while he is in the middle of singing *Malo*, and Britten never talks to him again.

Nearly three hours later the curtain falls to rapturous applause. It has been a triumph. The singers take their calls with becoming modesty, bowing, curtseying, again and again. Bouquets rain down upon the stage. Members of the orchestra, itself hardly bigger than a chamber ensemble, acknowledge their own plaudits, and Britten bows repeatedly, front, left and right, after replacing his baton neatly on the podium.

Back in England at the end of the long 700-mile return journey, she is consumed by restlessness and a growing dissatisfaction with what she now views as the unacceptable confines of her daily life. The trip to Venice was a turning point, Far from satisfying her obsession, it has actively fed it. Her commitment is now stronger than ever.

She starts to chafe against the missed opportunities to see even more concerts and performances of his works as they tour the country, to resent the limits the school terms and her teaching duties impose on her notional freedom. She needs ever more time to delve into the librettos of his operas, the poetry used in his choral works and canticles, because she knows these speak to her and through them the composer himself. She has recognized the messages encoded in his music and captured in the lyrics, lyrics like the beautiful lines in his *Wedding Anthem*, lyrics that feed into the growing conviction that she is his chosen partner. The fact that the words were written by another is irrelevant: the connection is seamless.

Shortly after her return she takes the train down to London to see the opera's British premier, this time with the Sadler's Wells Opera. By now she knows it almost by heart, and the dark forces that drive the story have become ever more compelling. The walk from Holborn's tube station to the theatre is already familiar. The wheels of looming red double-decker buses hiss in the rain, and drivers hoot furiously at the black cabs that stop abruptly in their path to drop off or pick up passengers, turning on a sixpence. A gust of wind tugs at her umbrella, threatening to blow it inside out. It's all a far cry from the canals of Venice, but soon she is inside the theatre and absorbed in the same immersive world of the opera, transported back into a sinister landscape where two children become victims and the ghosts become monsters.

Her sense of her bond with its composer becomes a conviction the same evening when she finally meets him face to face outside the stage door. She has been waiting there on the pavement ever since the performance ended and the curtain came down for the last time, shivering against the cold in the by now habitual hope of seeing him and getting his autograph.

The scene is one that has been repeated time and again in different places, different cities, outside different concert halls, but previously she has always held back at the last minute, fearful of being ignored, of being invisible.

This time she asserts herself, emboldened by opportunity, thrusting her programme and pen almost under his nose as she pushes herself to the front of the small and hopeful group of people waiting, like her, for the chance to meet their idol in person.

As he takes the pen, her pen, and his hand brushes against

hers she feels the warmth of his skin, senses the beat of his blood pulsing in his wrist, and breathes in his smell. When his eyes look into hers as he returns the signed programme she knows she is, for him, the only person in the world. It is a moment that she will replay endlessly, a moment she remembers as a moment of pure communion.

But despite the signature that proves the encounter took place, she still feels anxious, vulnerable, plagued by doubts about whether he has space in his life for her after all, and the need for a connection that goes beyond watching him from an anonymous seat in the stalls becomes ever more insistent. Shortly afterwards she resigns from her teaching job, telling her parents she needs a break. The daily stress of living is affecting her health. She has trouble sleeping, she's feeling depressed again. She needs to spend more time in London, a city rich in the culture she craves, the place where she can recover and make plans for the future. She buys the recording of the opera and spends hours listening to it, reliving the Venice trip every time. The priest's wandering hand becomes conflated with the touch of the composer's hand as he returned her pen.

Mindful of their daughter's frailty, her parents reluctantly agree to give her an allowance to tide her over while she recovers her equilibrium before returning to her Huddersfield teaching job once she feels better.

What they cannot know is that they have unwittingly given her a passport, and the time, to becoming a full-blown stalker.

I have left the school and am able at last to devote my time to him. Best of all, I am in London, and going to so many concerts that I feel giddy. The Marylebone bedsit is central, close to the tube and buses. No more interminable train journeys back to Huddersfield, and late-night taxis. It is wonderful, rhapsodic. I know he remembers our meeting – how could he forget. That feeling of mutual recognition was unmistakable. I saw it in his eyes and felt its power, like an electric current running through my body.

As I watched him writing his name on my programme with the same hand that had written the music I had just finished listening to, I was filled with a feeling of absolute certitude that we are meant for each other at the deepest of levels. The messages are there, waiting for me. I have looked inside myself and have found the answers.

If my life is to have meaning I must fulfill my destiny.

I am his. He is mine.

CHAPTER 9

Festival opening

The composer is now the woman's life, her inspiration and her vocation. Their eyes have met, and she knows indisputably that he feels the same way, that she has read the messages aright, the messages encoded in his music, messages she returns to again and again:

> These two are not two
> Love has made them one
> Amo Ergo Sum![9]

Her heart pounds when she thinks of him and at times she fears she will suffocate with the intensity of her emotions as her chest constricts. The joy is exhilarating. Suddenly every day is filled with sunshine and opportunity. Meaning and purpose have been restored to her life and the cloud of depression has lifted. The old panic attacks when she doubts whether she is worthy of his love still recur, but they are no longer debilitating. She sees clearly the way forward at last.

He is, of course, unable to reply to the postcards and letters she has been sending, because she has been far too clever. She knows already that the so-called friends who surround him like wasps will be jealous and possessive, that they will stop at nothing to come between them because they are determined to keep him to themselves. The fictitious address she has used since moving to London is a stroke of genius, ensuring she cannot be tracked down. It is enough to know that fate has predestined them to be together, and that this is a shared truth. She has read the messages hidden in his works and she is ready to return his love. How else to interpret them?

It is now imperative that she tells him she understands the meaning his messages carry for her alone, and that she responds in kind. In a moment of pure compassion and loving amity she writes to him to let him know that she recognizes their engagement, that she is happy to become his fiancée. But again there can be no reply. He needs more. She must reassure him, comfort him, make him feel safe, loved, adored, embedded in her heart and in her soul. In an excess of almost spiritual elation she writes to him again. She is his bride, his spiritual and physical partner. They are now married in a holy communion.

She imagines herself in bridal white, a priest's unctuous tones of blessing, the feel of the ring being slipped on to her finger, Mendelssohn's triumphant wedding march, then the honeymoon in some vague Elysian setting; a room diffused with the softest of sunlight, motes of fairy dust dancing in the air, her lover, now her husband, approaching her from a window looking out onto an idyllic view of slender green cypresses amid rolling hills bathed in warmth and beauty. The time has come for her life and his to be conjoined. The fantasy is without any sexual element at all.

Of course I haven't give the correct address on my letters. Why? Because otherwise I will be hunted down and stopped. His friends will always be false friends. I know, because that's what happens when someone like him becomes famous. It's the price he pays –

surrounded by sycophants, hangers-on, leeches. They will always be jealous because they will never understand his need for my love and support. They cannot tolerate the thought of losing their hold on him. They will do everything in their power to prevent him from having someone in his life who means more to him than they do. They are incapable of sharing him, of letting him find love apart, which is why he has had to send me messages in secret. They are bent on controlling his life, they feed off his fame, like parasites, like vultures around a carcass. But he is more alive than anyone I have ever met.

Why else is he sending me messages that only I can detect and understand. The divine Donne sonnets, Lucretia's entrance. We are both locked in lives that prevent us from achieving the joy and love we deserve. I am his path to freedom, and when he is free he will achieve even greater creativity and renown. My role in this is crucial. I am his saviour. I am his wife.

Ever since that meeting outside the London theatre she has not stopped scheming and making plans to go to Aldeburgh, driven by the need to see him, to feel his touch once more. In a moment of inspiration she asks herself what better time to visit than during the annual Aldeburgh Festival. Founded by Britten and Pears seven years earlier, the Festival has by now become an established fixture on the national arts scene. It will provide the ideal opportunity to meet again. Her decision is cemented when she discovers that the key event will be three performances of *The Turn of the Screw,* conducted by the composer – the opera she saw in Venice, and then again in London, less than a year ago.

June is one of the loveliest months in England, and the Festival dates have been chosen wisely. In June the leaves on the trees still retain traces of their springtime luminosity, and the sprawling grain fields of East Anglia are a sea of emerald green. Festival signs and posters advertising fringe events, lectures, exhibitions, recitals, will soon festoon a town already in thrall to the hectic, febrile atmosphere that will transform its day-to-day identity for this one week of the year, and feed off its own energy. It beckons with growing urgency.

She reads the Henry James story again in readiness, and revisits the reviews of the Venice premiere and the journal entries she wrote at the time. How the critics agreed it was a triumph, the way its somber mood chimed with the dank miasma that blankets the water-logged city in winter, a story of the corruption of innocence, good versus evil, the governess versus the evil Quint, and the two lost souls, Miles and Flora. Every scene remains burned in her memory. She imagines herself offering redemption, elevated by her love for the opera's composer, by the love they share.

Preparations include reserving a room in a bed and breakfast well in advance, mindful of the fact that otherwise she will have nowhere to stay at a time when accommodation is at a premium. She has already arranged to arrive two days before the Festival starts.

In between she will wander the town and immerse herself in the atmosphere, listen to the lectures, go to Festival films and art exhibitions, and above all visit Crag House to see for herself where he lives and works. She envisages him welcoming her with open arms, introducing her to the world as his wife. Soon sheets of foolscap are littering her desk and filling the wastepaper basket. Mrs Benjamin Britten – the words cover page after page as she practises her new signature, writing it over and over, concentrating on the shared initials that will confirm her status and mark her out as his. Different pens, different inks. Blue, black, peacock green. The dramatic curlicues lend the letters grace and dignity, giving them a timeless quality.

CHAPTER 10

Crag House

The sun is shining in Aldeburgh when she gets off the train, and the air is crystalline clear. So much to see, so much to absorb, taste and feel. On impulse, after checking into her boarding house she takes a walk along the town's beach, rejoicing in the sound her feet make as they crunch against the millions of small pebbles that shift and move underfoot, sparkling in the light as the waves recede. Seagulls swoop overhead, wheeling in the sky above, and she can smell and taste the fresh salt tang on the air. Anything and everything seems possible.

    From there it's a short walk to the art galleries and churches, guided by the map she picked up at the station entrance. She's keen to see where performances will be taking place and is revelling in the adventure, on the verge of seizing control of her future at last. She discovers that a wine festival is taking place the next evening, an annual Festival event. Then time at last to visit Crag House, the place where he eats, lives and breathes, where he rises from bed every morning, sleeps every night. She has been putting it off on purpose, wallowing in the bliss of anticipation, delaying the treat for maximum impact, disciplining her desire to the point where she thinks she will explode. It is virtually next door to where the opera will be staged, the Jubilee Hall,

Standing opposite it on the Crab Path frontage, she feels as starstruck as a teenager, and physically closer than at any time since the night when he signed her programme and looked into her eyes. She studies the sprawling house carefully, noting windows, doors, pathways, peers over the wall at the untidy garden and cane chairs, then doubles back on her footsteps to see it anew from the other side.

I am back at my bed and breakfast after seeing his house. So much to absorb, so much to think about. It was like some dream, like looking into my future, but the landlady accosted me instead. She is large and friendly in the usual inquisitive way, and extremely voluble. She talks about the Festival incessantly. I cannot get a word in edgeways, even if I wanted to. Listening to her babble on I see how proud the town is of its Festival, and even prouder of its famous residents, the two men who founded the festival and made it all possible. Here they are treated like heroes.

When she starts talking about him I find myself hanging on to every word. I long to hear as much about him as possible, hugging to myself the sound of his name as I fight the urge to let her know that we are secretly married. But I know I must be patient and let him chose the time and place. It has to be soon though, because I cannot go on living with this secret for much longer.

Besides, my secret is not for everyone, least of all this good-natured but garrulous woman with her sharp eyes. I doubt whether she has ever heard his music in her life. If she only knew! Imagine her astonishment, how impressed she would be, how she would look at me with awe and respect and see me as he does.

This woman is not all deference however. Indeed she's distinctly less enthusiastic about the other visitors; the crowds that descend during Festival time, the out-of-towners. They may have money to burn, and of course the townsfolk aren't going to say no to their money, but it doesn't mean we have to like them, she says. If I go to the wine festival the next evening I'll be able to see for myself. She's especially scornful about their pretensions and snobbery, and their patronizing ways. Mr Britten's always there, she adds, but he's different. I know what she means.

She rolls her eyes upwards in time-honoured fashion as she shares her views, and carries on gossiping. Did I know that Mr Britten and Mr Pears had been conscientious objectors during the war, she continued, eyeing me to gauge my reaction. I pretended to be surprised and looked at her enquiringly. By then she was in full flow, unable to resist carrying on, even though she sounded cautious when she mentioned they went to America for a while.

Then she brightened up again as she told me how they came back to help share the burden of war and play their part, despite disapproving of war so strongly. They may have been conchies but they came through in the end, didn't they.

She hates war too, like every right thinking Englishman, but the Germans had to be resisted because otherwise England would have become part of Germany. And after all, they started it. And serve them right too. They got what they deserved.

It's all been exhausting. When she talked about Ben I was ready to listen, but I don't have the time to listen to her droning on about the war. I had to get rid of her so I said I had a headache and went back to my room. I have more plans to make.

The next morning she makes a decision that is scarcely her own any more. She must go back to Crag House, but this time she won't just look over the wall or through the gaps in the fence around the garden. This time she will go into the house itself.

It must be a time when no one is at home, when the two men are out and she can roam at will. They are already aware that there have been intruders, and were shocked when they discovered the initials scored into the back of one of the dining room chairs, but the house is old and not secure.

From her hidden position opposite she watches and waits. Her caution is rewarded when they emerge from the garden gate, both wearing white tennis flannels. She has heard that Britten is an excellent tennis player and keenly competitive, that he hates to lose. Snatches of their banter float back to her as they walk off in the direction of the nearby tennis court, rackets swinging from their hands in easy unison. Pears is handsome, taller. She feels a sharp stab of jealousy at the sight of her rival.

It proves absurdly easy to get inside through an unlocked back door. Nonetheless she still knocks cautiously as she enters to double check she has the place to herself, but there is no response. The house is empty, with the muffled deadness that signals absence. She looks back over her shoulder one last time before sidling inside, guided by the photographs she has cut out from the feature about Britten and Pears she found three years ago in a popular women's magazine, photographs showing the house's interior and its layout. At present they are lying on the floor of her boarding house room, spread out for reference. She knows exactly where she wants to go.

Her motives are mixed, confused. What she's doing is wrong, it amounts to trespass, she could get caught. But the compulsion to find out more about him and to physically enter into his private life – a life she is entitled to share as his lover, his wife – is overriding and she's powerless to deny it.

In the main hallway she looks up at the wide staircase facing her, listens again to make doubly sure she is alone, then ascends it slowly, step by step, to the first floor landing. Her hands linger on the bannister rail, eking out every moment so she can absorb and experience the enormity of what she is doing. Her heart is pounding. For a moment she fears she is about to faint.

At the turn of the staircase she has to pause so she can draw in a huge lungful of air and regain control of her breathing. The paintings lining the walls look down on her disdainfully as if blinded by their frames to her intrusion. A portrait in muted earth tones shows a younger Britten sitting in three-quarter view, elbows resting on the arms of the chair, long fingers clasped together over his lap. The eyes don't match: the gaze of the furthest one drifts disconcertingly to the right. It makes him look aloof, unfocussed, disconnected. He should be looking at her instead.

The first room she enters must be his office. A large window looks out over the sea and a dark upright piano fills a corner. Framed black and white photographs of productions of previous operas hang on the walls. Directly in front of the window is a desk topped with green leather, a space in the middle for the writer's knees. She goes over and sits on the hard chair, stretching her palms across the desk's surface.

She flicks through the orderly papers, tries some of the drawers, opens notebooks, studies some pages intently as if seeking vital information, even though she is not sure what she is looking for. Next to what appears to be a working score she picks up a copy of *A Midsummer Night's Dream*. At an earmarked page she finds what can only be another message left for her, proof if ever needed that he knew she would come, and has been expecting her:

> If then true lovers ever have been cross'd
> It stands as an edict in destiny
> Then let us teach our trial patience.[10]

Then she spots the postcards, the ones she has sent, stacked in a tidy pile on the left-hand side of the desk. Another sign. He has kept them in front of him on purpose and left them out for her see, proof of how much they mean to them.

There is Ophelia, floating serenely on her back, hair drifting in the water, a pale upraised hand clasping a delicate sprig of wild flowers as she consents to her destiny. In another Christ stands at a door with a lantern in his hand. His gentle eyes are sorrowful and compassionate, full of infinite understanding. The vigorous chisel-shaped beard confers a compensating masculinity and authority. No wonder the disciples followed him so slavishly and the crowds flocked to listen to him before falling upon the loaves and fishes.

A third shows a man and woman sitting side by side in the prow of a boat, bound for a new life together, their gaze fixed steadfastly on an unknown future as the present is consigned to the past. The white cliffs of Dover shimmer in the distance; a tiny hand clasping the woman's is all that can be seen of the baby hidden inside her shawl. The picture of the Bridge of Sighs with its Italian stamp is a heart-stopping reminder of Venice, conjuring up Casanova crossing the bridge on his way to the palace's dank, rat-infested dungeons.

She turns the cards over, re-reading the messages she has sent. At first she had simply let him know how much she admired him, then the joy she found in going to his concerts and recitals and listening to his works.

She singles out the card written after the fateful encounter outside the Sadler's Wells stage door, the one when she told him how much their meeting had meant to her, how she would always remember the way he looked deep into her eyes.

'I have learnt to recognize your messages,' she had written. 'I'm indescribably happy to learn that you love me too.'

And on another, 'I have photographs of you pinned to every wall, and cannot stop looking at them. I love your eyes, your hair, your face, your hands, and most of all your genius. We were made for each other.'

The messages continue, each an escalation of the previous one: 'I know we are engaged. I know now how to interpret the words of your canticles, the messages you send me. They are beautiful. I accept.'

And last of all she finds the letter where she reassured him, writing that she recognized she was now his wife because that was what fate had decreed. He has kept them all, the cards, the letters, cherished them; her love is reciprocated. Time for another message, and what better than that same sublime Canticle verse again. She takes out her pen and leaves a final postcard on his desk, written in the now familiar hand that he will instantly recognize:

> Ev'n like two little bank-divided brooks,
> That wash the pebbles with their wanton streams
> And having raged and searched a thousand nooks
> Meet both at length at silver-breasted Thames,
> Where in a greater current they conjoin,
> So I my best beloved's am,
> So he is mine.[11]

But there is still more. With a start she recalls herself to her surroundings. It is time to get up from the desk before someone returns and continue with her explorations. Off the landing an adjoining door opens onto a bedroom, comfortably if unremarkably furnished apart from a surprising and narrow single bed. The magazine photographs help her identify it as Peter Pears' bedroom. It looks like a bachelor's room. It holds little of interest for her.

She moves on, halts at another door that leads into a pristine white bathroom – Ben's surely. Inside the large cabinet fixed over the basin she finds a shaving soap container and matching brush. Slowly and deliberately she strokes her cheeks with the softly pliant badger hairs, pictures him drawing his razor up and over his throat, hearing the sound of its rasp against his chin.

The next room is even smaller, clearly a bedroom again, but with clothing that can only belong to a child, and a boy at that, folded on the seat of a plain wooden chair. More clothes threaten to escape from a leather suitcase lying on the floor. She shakes her head in puzzlement, disconcerted, wondering how to absorb what she has seen. Later the memory will return to trouble her, but for the present she pushes aside what she has seen and continues on her way.

Then back to what must be his bedroom, next door to the office. She takes in the large double bed that dominates the space, pauses for long seconds before approaching the dressing table and picking up a silver-backed hairbrush, then draws it slowly through her hair as she looks at her reflection in the mirror, imagining him standing behind her, taking the brush gently from her hand, putting his arms around her waist. She turns, brush still in hand, and walks back across the landing and down the staircase, brushing her hair all the while, unable to put it down. The air crackles with static and single strands float up in the air like a halo, throwing out flickers of light.

In the large sitting room downstairs there is a harpsichord and a grand piano, its lid up, ready to play. Crossing over to it she sits down and picks out a simple nursery rhyme tune with her right hand, *Twinkle, Twinkle Little Star*, adding a mournful base line in a minor key before getting to her feet again and wandering around the room, looking at the furniture, picking up the cushions, studying the photographs and paintings, works by John Piper, Walter Sickert, pausing before a small Constable pastoral.

Other pictures show stage and costume designs she recognizes from the operas she has been to. A silver salver and half a dozen bottles sit on top of a well-stocked drinks cabinet alongside crystal decanters with porcelain medallions hanging from their necks on thin silver chains – whisky, brandy, sherries. She pictures him pouring her a glass of palest Fino before sitting at the piano and playing a piece for her, the two of them playing one of his duets together, laughing together in domestic harmony. His hands will look like bells as they dance over the keys. His shoulder will press against hers and transmit the warmth of his body one to another.

The peace is suddenly broken by a noise towards the rear of the house, the unmistakable sound of a door opening, startling her out of her reverie. She jumps up in alarm: who can it be, what if she's caught? Peering round the door, she catches a glimpse of a woman at the end of the hallway with a basket of groceries on the floor at her feet. She listens, pressed up tight against the side of the piano as the housekeeper clumps towards the kitchen, then tiptoes back down the hallway before leaving as noiselessly as she had entered. She dare not risk discovery; only Ben is capable of understanding why she had to be there, why she was only obeying his summons.

As she closes the back door and retreats back down the path, her mission accomplished, she feels closer to the composer and his life than ever before.

I feel elated. The day has been wonderful and I am blissfully aware of the afternoon sun on my face. I have succeeded. I have been in his home and found the postcards I sent and the messages that prove he was expecting me. I have seen where he works and where he sleeps.

My mind has also been put to rest, thank goodness, on a matter that I must admit had been worrying me. I will be frank for once, and confess how relieved I was when I saw that he and his friend – I will call him PP from now on – have separate bedrooms. Ridiculous I know, but sometimes it's been difficult to ignore the rumours that their friendship is too close, even unnatural, and I've been wracked with doubt. I feel ashamed now that I ever felt like this. They may live and work together, but that is all. I was ridiculously afraid I would find something compromising, but nothing. Nothing at all. It is all spiteful and loathsome. They are obviously the closest of friends, even the dearest of friends, but I am the one he loves. The messages prove it.

But what about the boy's clothes I found in one of the other bedrooms, because I know he doesn't have any children. That did surprise me, until I remembered that he has a godson who comes to stay sometimes. That explains it. I have read that he loves children, and I know some of his finest works have been written especially for them. So doesn't this make him an even finer person?

Towards the end, though, when the woman returned, I thought she was going to discover me and I had to hide, just in case she looked in, or came in to dust, or polish, or whatever it is that housekeepers do. Foolish I know, but how would I have explained why I was there? It doesn't bear thinking about and I'm aghast for a moment at the risk I took. If she hadn't been concentrating on closing the door and dealing with the shopping she could have caught me.

But I didn't have a choice, did I? And besides, it's my right. I'm not like all those others who sneak in without permission out of common and vulgar curiosity. I'm Ben's wife, and soon he will have the chance to acknowledge it. I'm hoping it will be this evening. God willing. Then his friends and all those others who think they are so sophisticated and clever, and place such selfish demands on his precious attention, will have to accept me. Idle, shallow gossip. Evil even. He is too good for them, too good for them all. All I need is patience.

CHAPTER 11

Wine and roses

By the time she arrives at the wine festival the moon is already hanging like a premature ghost of itself in the sky, pinned there by a trick of light in the evening sunshine, waiting for night time to assert itself. The atmosphere is heady, seductive, incestuous.

At the entrance to the grounds she pauses to take her bearings. It's been an awkward journey – nine miles by taxi. Home county accents ring out shrilly as well-dressed men and women exchange noisy greetings, and sartorial eccentricities are on garish display as competing egos vie for visibility in this high culture battle zone. It is the prelapsarian decade when breathalyzers have yet to be invented, a time when drunken driving is still a celebration of adulthood and heavy drinking a hallmark of hedonism.

She is intimidated, unnerved by so much display and swagger, but still buoyed up from the morning's adventure when she saw where he eats, lives, sleeps and breathes. Her landlady had assured her he will be present as usual. After all it's an institution by now she had added, the informal start to the Festival proper.

With an effort she forces herself to walk across the newly mown grass and over to the marquee. She urgently needs a glass of wine before braving the chattering groups. It is immediately apparent that all the great and the good of Aldeburgh are there, circulating amongst the tables set up for medocs, sauternes, burgundies and champagne under the banner of the Wine Lovers' Society. The aura of collective confidence is almost overwhelming.

For a moment she has to fight an impulse to flee. She has no place here, she lacks any connection with her surroundings, she's hopeless at small talk, she is making a terrible mistake, why did she come? But then she remembers – Ben is going to be there, and her resolve returns. She no longer feels fearful and out of place. She is instead a privileged person apart because she possesses a secret that belongs to her and one other person only. Her anonymity is her protection. She will listen and learn, and then she will see him again because she knows he is here, waiting for her.

Fortified by a second glass, she walks over towards a couple locked in a private conversation. She has no intention of joining them. Instead she will discreetly position herself nearby. She has already cast herself in the role of spectator rather than participant, and the opportunity to eavesdrop is compelling.

The man and woman are standing under a tree at a careful distance from the other groups. They appear to be in the middle of an intense exchange that sets them apart. She hears the man ask the woman what her festival role is this year. The question is trite – conventional small talk, but his mouth is twisted in a tight smile devoid of conviction and his eyes look like bruised holes.

'Didn't you know? I've become one of the corpses,' the woman replies, looking away. Her face has clouded, and the wry, sardonic tone echoes the man's enquiry, carries the same message of embittered rejection. 'He devours people. He can only love or hate. Once someone's no more use to him he spews out was left.'

The impression of some dark shared experience is confirmed by his response: 'Ah yes, moths getting too close to the flame.'

It is all mystifying. What are they talking about – surely it can't be her Ben? She catches sight of him in the distance, working the crowd. Even from where she is she can tell he is in top form, and his charisma is clear. The women in particular seem to adore him, attracted to him like moths to a flame. So that's what they were talking about: she pictures one of the gross furred insects flying closer and ever closer to a hot, burning candle, whirling until its wings shrivel, scorched by the heat, and the fat downy body plummets sizzling to the ground. Is that what the woman meant, that her lover's friends and admirers end up as corpses? And if so, what are the implications for her?

With a shiver she pushes away the thought and turns to another group, her attention caught by the sight of a man she recognizes as Peter Pears talking to the composer Michael Tippett. The distinctive profile is a giveaway. As she watches, Britten detaches himself from a woman in mid-sentence and walks over to join them. Pears nods briefly in acknowledgement before continuing his anecdote. He is in full flow.

'Benji,' she hears him exclaim warmly, 'Michael and I were just telling the priceless story about Lucretia in Italy. As I was saying, just as the rape was about to begin, the curtain stuck. And there was poor Tarquinius, utterly at a loss.'

As if on cue Tippett delivers the punchline. 'And then suddenly there were shouts from the audience, Coraggio! Coraggio!'

She watches Pears join in the ensuing laughter, popular, charismatic, boisterously self-regarding. It was marvellous, he declaims, his eyes alert to his audience's response, watchful, assessing their appreciation. It is obviously a story he has told before and is ready to tell again. But his braying mirth is not shared by Britten who has turned away, frowning his disapproval.

This is her chance: she steps forward quickly and intercepts him. The reference to Lucretia has supplied her with the opportunity she has been waiting for. At last they are face to face and she seizes the moment, aware that she has come to a crossroads, that it is now or never.

'I particularly appreciated the setting of the interlude while the rape was actually happening,' she hears herself blurting out. The words sound foolish to her ears as they tumble over each other. It is a risky gambit, all wrong she senses; she has already seen his face close in distaste when listening to Pears' vulgar tale a minute ago.

Conscious that she is skirting dangerous territory, she hastily expands with a further quotation: 'The rhythm of the orchestra is such a deep contradiction to what is being said, "Nothing impure survives, all passion perishes."'[12]

Then pulling herself together extends her hand, adding, 'Oh, by the way, I'm one of your greatest admirers.'

He appears disconcerted by what she has said, but takes her hand in return and replies politely, expertly drawing upon reserves of well-honed experience. 'How do you do. You're obviously a discerning audience.' But why hasn't he recognized her? She continues, fighting down a mounting desperation:

> To dare to part,
> For we are of one another
> And between us, there is one love as we loved
> was to be never but as moiety.[13]

He must recognize the words. He must. How can he fail to do so? She had written them on one of the cards she found on his desk. She had seen it sitting there. Surely the time she has been waiting for has come. He smiles again, but there is no glimmer of recognition in return, no spark of empathy. Nothing. In the awkward silence that follows she struggles for what to say next, to reveal to him that she is his wife, that she has come for him, but it is too late.

The moment is interrupted, destroyed on the brink of its

birth by a confident, proprietorial woman who strides up and takes him possessively by the arm, calling him Ben, explaining that she has someone who is dying to meet him. But just before walking away he looks back at her and completes the quote, incapable of resisting the incipient vanity that afflicts the famous, the unavoidable adjunct of their heightened self-regard.

> To love as we loved was to die, daily with
> anxiety; to love as we loved was to live
> on the edge of tragedy.[14]

Afterwards, he is thankful he was rescued from the strange encounter. Although he's quite sure he's never met the woman before, he cannot cast off a nagging sense that she is somehow more than just another admirer with the usual encyclopaedic knowledge his fans have of his works. The disquiet is fleeting however, soon forgotten in the greetings that carry on competing for his attention. He must leave soon in any case, the morning's tennis match has tired him and he is exhausted by rehearsals. Tomorrow night he is on the podium, conducting the opening performance of *The Turn of the Screw*. He needs time to rest and prepare. So many demands, so many people depending on him, so many obligations, expectations. If it weren't for Peter's support it would all be intolerable. It is only later, when he discovers what has been left on his desk, that he realises his unknown admirer has turned into something much more sinister. Suddenly his study feels like a trap, a sanctuary no longer.

Alone again, she lingers on feeling deserted, bereft, consumed by a rage with the woman who has just robbed her of her chance, by a mounting hatred of everyone there and their easy assumptive access to his life, access she has just been denied. The weather changes suddenly, and within minutes a wind has blown up and the clouds gather, darkening the skies. People start to disperse, hurriedly gulping down the last of their wine, checking for umbrellas as the first drops of rain begin to fall, scurrying to the car park. She will be drenched and chilled by the time she has found a taxi for the return journey, but her resolve is undiminished. There are imperatives she cannot deny.

CHAPTER 12

The Invasion

Back in her room she takes off her dripping clothes and sits on the narrow bed shivering, her face working in visible distress. The day had appeared to promise so much, and for a brief time she had believed its promise would come true. The cruelty of that interruption stokes the anger, the resentment. The woman had come with a purpose, another false friend in the gilded circle, another enemy determined to deny him the happiness he deserves. Once she's changed into dry clothes she goes for a solitary meal down a nearby side street, then heads back to her lodgings to write up her journal. The break has given her time to review the day's events, to go over every detail obsessively and examine again and again what had happened, to dwell on where had it all gone so wrong.

We met, but why didn't he recognize me. Or maybe he did, and was on the very verge of embracing me. Maybe that was what the message meant, the one he left on his desk waiting for me to read, the one saying we must be patient:

> *If then true lovers ever have been cross'd*

> *It stands as an edict in destiny*
> *Then let us teach our trial patience.*[15]

Of course – that explains why he pretended not to recognize me. He must be waiting for the right time to tell the world about us. I understand. I always understand. But I cannot go on understanding for ever. After all, he started this – is he just leading me on? No that's impossible, he's too good for that. I will strive to be patient like he says, but oh, it is so difficult, because I have been patient for too long already and it is becoming unsupportable.

I have come all this way specially to see him, because I have my rights too. I am terrified our chance of true happiness will pass, that it will evaporate, killed before its birth, killed by time and my own failures, and that another may take my place if I don't act now. The very thought makes me seethe with frustration. And yes, with a rage that makes my blood boil. How can I live without him. I must give him another chance to say he returns my love, because I know that is what he is also seeking. My anguish is his anguish and I am starting to realise what has to be done. It will take all my courage, but I have a duty to us both. I cannot let our love wither for want of action. I am ready for whatever it takes.

I heard them talking about him behind his back, talking of corpses, who is in, and who is out. Idle, shallow gossip. Evil even. He is too good for them, too good for them all. All I need is patience. And the courage to do what I have to. I will never join the corpses.

But when she puts her pen down her mind is still in turmoil and sleep is impossible. She decides to go for a late walk rather than face the long barren small hours that every insomniac dreads. It is close to midnight when she leaves, but the landlady has given her a key. She can come and go as she pleases.

Outside she looks up at the intermittent moon, one side already dimmed and on the wane. Soon it will be little more than a crescent sliver and then nothing, as if it never existed. Only the tides will prove it is still there, pulling the oceans from side to side, steering great waves and currents from pole to pole. The rain has abated to a few drops but the clouds remain, shifting restlessly in thrall to invisible winds, scudding across the night sky. She had meant to walk into town, away from the beach, but finds her feet leading her inexorably in the opposite direction, back towards Crag House. It exerts a pull like a magnet that she's powerless to resist. All over the town shops are closed, restaurants and pubs have emptied, and the streets are deserted apart from an elderly couple and their dog huddled on a corner. The people of Aldeburgh are asleep, safe in their beds, safe in their secure domestic lives.

When she reaches the Hall she looks up at the unlit windows next door before going down the side path towards the sea. She has had to return. She has no choice. And she knows she can see the house as well, better in fact, from the beach side as from the front.

From the corner of one of the huts opposite she rakes the house with her eyes, wondering which room he is in, what he is doing, what he ate for dinner, whether he has been rehearsing, whether he saw the message she left for him on his desk, whether he is thinking of her. But the windows remain blank save for a faint light shining from the highest one; its drawn curtains hide the room behind, revealing nothing. She pauses, then walks down the beach seeking more time, fighting the drag on her feet of the shifting pebbles, and then back again to resume her station, watching, listening, waiting.

Suddenly she ducks. She has heard the unmistakable sound from the house of the garden gate opening. Footsteps are coming down the path, softly at first, then louder as they come closer and closer. A figure appears, the figure of a man, towel in hand. It is Britten.

From her concealed hiding place her eyes follow him as he walks down to the edge of the sea, then looks around swiftly before taking off his robe. His pale buttocks gleam whitely in the moonlight. He is naked.

As he wades into the water she remembers reading about his love of night-time swims, of bathing nude. He has no idea he is being watched. When the water reaches waist height he submerges himself in one rapid movement and swims away powerfully, parallel to the shore. Then returns and re-emerges, shaking the water from his head, running his hands over his face. She sees the dark hair at his groin, and his sex, before he dries himself quickly and puts his robe on again. She holds herself tightly as he walks up the beach back towards the gate leading into the Crag House garden, flattening herself again against the wall, scarcely daring to breath. Her feelings are in tumult. It is the first time she has been confronted with his unadorned physicality, and the sight will return again and again. Part of her is repelled, and her romantic notions feel assailed, even violated. Then she sees that this is indeed part of what being a wife means. He has reached out to her. She will surrender when the time comes.

The next morning she stays in bed as long as possible, resisting the clock in an agony of deferral before remembering the stained glass lecture she's read about, anything to fill the time, and the peal of bells at one of the church towers – she's forgotten which one. The memories of the past twenty-four hours are swirling in her head, crowding her mind, creating further confusion as she struggles to process her reaction to what she saw. For a moment she rues her sexual inexperience before taking comfort from the thought that this sophisticated urbane man who has sought her out, who has sent her so many messages, who conjures music from the spheres, will teach her and guide her once everyone knows they are man and wife in the fullest sense.

The day passes in a blur of sounds she barely registers, of people she scarcely sees, views she scarcely notices. The rain returns, unseasonal, quiet, steady and persistent. Photographs of the Crag House interiors still litter her bedroom floor. She knows the title of the opera holds the message she has been waiting for. Time to start getting ready for the Jubilee Hall, time for the next chapter to begin.

She has planned her actions carefully and shudders with exaltation and anticipation. This is one of the bravest things she has ever done. It is also one of the truest, and one of the most necessary. If he had only come to her as she had asked, had only acknowledged her as his wife at the wine festival, things could have been otherwise. But now she has no choice. How else to convince him, to make the scales fall from his eyes, to make him see the depth of her love, to make him hold out his arms and embrace her into his life and his genius.

As she dresses she caresses her body, imagining his hands sliding along her shoulder blades and across her breasts, his tongue hot and wet against the pulse beating in her neck. She has seen him naked, seen his white skin against the moonlight, and the recollection prompts a quick stab of desire that makes her gasp. The discovery of a capacity for lust jolts her disembodied romanticism in a way she never imagined. Whether Satan or Eros, it is meant to be.

Recollecting herself, she looks at her watch one last time and applies a final slash of lipstick. As she puts on her coat and twists the two silk scarves around her neck the anger returns, making her pull her gloves on sharply, tapping down the leather between the fingers, her mouth set. She is determined to put behind her the memory she has been trying to suppress, of a boy's clothes folded neatly on a chair and a suitcase lying on the floor of a child's bedroom, the vile rumours she's always ignored. She gets angry a lot now, more and more so. Sometimes it's because she is jealous. At other times she doesn't even know why.

Outside the rain has ceased, leaving glistening puddles that splash her shoes and drench her feet. Her heels tap sharply on the pavement as the hall comes into sight. The clouds have returned and the moon that shone above the beach the previous night remains hidden save for a faint nimbus of luminescence.

She checks her watch, but it is too early. She has miscalculated. The smattering of people at the hall's entrance are waiting for returned tickets, not for entry. Her courage falters. Then she remembers the public house she passed on her way and surrenders to a quick impulse, because the stress is almost more than she can bear. She retraces her footsteps, then hesitates outside before going in to order a drink. It is the first time she has been in a pub on her own. Women who go to public houses, or for that matter any kind of bar, have a certain reputation, but she is beyond caring, because she is desperate.

The hallmarks of a typical public house are all there, compressed into a long rectangular room dominated by the sour, stale smell of a beer-impregnated carpet, and spirals of cigarette smoke rising lazily from twisted butts in nicotine-stained ashtrays. The dim lighting emphasizes the shadows cast on tables where groups of men sit talking quietly to each other or nursing drinks on their own. In one corner two men are playing darts, expertly. They must be regulars. She almost turns and leaves as she absorbs the collective resistance to a woman without a man at her side, deterred by the surly barman who ignores her at first, making little effort to hide his disapproval as he directs her to a table on the far side of the room where she will be almost invisible. For a moment her resolve falters, but she is grimly determined and asks for a brandy.

The first sip makes her cough violently, spluttering as its rawness hits her throat. The couple at a nearby table look at her and back with an expression she intercepts. It's the smirk that does it: how dare they patronize her like that – who do they think they are?

Defiantly, she takes another sip, then another and another, and her shoulders loosen and relax as her belly warms in response.

But she is not a practised drinker and soon her head is spinning, gently at first as she swirls the amber liquid in the glass round and round in her hand, then more and more so, and the room starts swimming as the tears run down her cheeks, tears of sadness for a wasted day and a love that is testing her to the limit. Then it's a second glass, and a third, and her remaining grip on reality disappears as the alcohol takes over. Is she drinking to forget, or drinking to create an excuse that will prevent her from going through with a plan so fraught with risk. But what plan exactly? All she knows is that when he sees her again he will recognize her as his wife, and when their hands touch he will remember looking deep into her eyes and thank her for his salvation.

She rises unsteadily from her seat, nearly knocking it over, and demands a fourth glass, but this time the barman refuses to serve her. Looking at her watch again she is startled to see how late it is. Time has vanished, precious time when she should have been listening to the opera and watching him conduct. Is she too late? She fumbles in her bag for her lipstick, and smears on another layer. It makes her look like a clown. Mascara runs down her cheeks in ugly black streaks. The second half must be coming to its conclusion. There is not a moment to lose.

The barman is relieved to see her go, another drunk who can't control herself. What kind of woman comes into a pub on her own? He wouldn't let his wife do it. No way. And when she'd started blathering on to him that she was the composer's wife he knew she'd had enough. Everyone knows Mr Britten's not the marrying kind. We may not like it, but it is what it is. Besides, she was beginning to disturb the other customers. If she'd carried on like that he would have had to call the police. Or the ambulance if she'd fallen over. The floor's a hard place to land. She could have bumped her head and cut it open, and then matters would have been even worse. Mentally he pats himself on the back, satisfied he's done the right thing as he watches her walk unsteadily towards the door.

The alcohol has served its purpose however, and she is floating on Dutch courage, determined to see her plans through to their conclusion. But the details have become blurred, as blurred as her vision. She can no longer remember what the plan was.

Outside the hall entrance she pauses as she attempts to clear her head, to bring her surroundings into focus. But the main doors are closed, denying access. Then, recalling the stage door she had discovered earlier on, she stumbles down the side passage, splashing through the puddles, almost falling over as she lurches against a wall before recovering her balance. The door gives way easily when she turns the handle and slips inside. She is just in time. The final act is being played out with the boy, Miles, singing sweetly and terribly as the fatal story of manipulation and nemesis approaches its climax.

No one appears to stop her or challenge her presence. They are transfixed by what is happening on stage. From her place in the cramped wings she watches the closing scene before the curtain falls. She has always been invisible, and no more so than now when everyone is absorbed in the opera's terrible denouement. She steps out of the way, almost falling over as the performers hurry back on stage to take their curtain calls and bow to the wildly applauding audience. For a moment she is at a loss as to what to do next, and wonders how, and why, she is here.

Then suddenly, inexplicably, she finds herself amongst them, pushing past the soloists as they go to take another curtain call, standing opposite Ben. Her Ben. Her husband. She hears a harsh shrieking sound. Someone is calling out again and again, 'Ben, Oh Ben…Ben, oh Ben,' and she is startled and shocked by the tumult behind the words. He stands a few feet away on his podium staring at her, immobilised in horror.

Slowly she becomes aware of the source of the cries as her

throat rasps with pain and her ears ring. Gasping, she turns to run as hands take her arms, tugging, pulling urgently, roughly, grabbing hold of her, hurting. Dimly realising that she is in the grip of some awful, ungovernable force, she allows herself to be hustled off the stage, her body shuddering as she gives way to huge, gulping sobs.

CHAPTER 13

The Meeting

I think I have gone mad. What is happening me? I feel like two people with two personalities – one sane and rational, the other a stranger who has stolen my identity and taken over control, leaving me watching myself helplessly from the sidelines. I am powerless to resist this version of myself even though I recognize it is a form of madness. I have become my own witness to a version of myself that I cannot control, and I am desperately afraid of what I will do next.

I keep on seeing his face – the shock and horror on it. I understand. But he should have recognized me before, at the wine festival. I could see he recognized me once I was facing him. And I know now that he will never forget me again. I have made sure of that. Perhaps he will understand at last how much I love him, and will forgive me and come for me. I have learned where and how he leaves his messages, and maybe the look on his face was a look of self discovery; when he saw how much he loves me too.

Or have I made a terrible, terrible mistake? Have I been mistaken all along? Have I become one of the corpses too? No, that's not possible. It can't be. He loves me. He has told me so in so many ways. I was only doing what he wished, showing the world I loved him in return.

I also understand now what happened to Miles, and to the

governess, and fear this is happening to me too. If there was a Quint I could find a way of escaping, and even save myself without having to die like Miles did. But there is only my Ben, and he has to be a force for good. I am trapped in a terrible quandary from which there is no escape. I have to follow my fate, because there is only one way forward. My future is now out of my hands. I have to submit to whatever happens next because I am trapped in my insanity – for this is what I realise it is. At the same time I have never felt more sane in my life. What have I left to lose?

Her family are fully involved by now, as appalled as anyone by the unfolding horror of their sister's madness, her mental instability and illness, for what else can it be. When the brother calls the older sister later the next morning to let her know what happened, they try and work out where it all went so terribly wrong.

He was there with his wife he explains, sitting in the hall when it happened. They go to the Festival every year – it's not far from their home, and they had read the glowing reviews after the opera's Sadler's Wells premiere. They were full of comfortable anticipation, excited at the prospect of seeing Britten conduct at the height of his fame and hearing Peter Pears in person. And the performance had delivered on every promise until the disastrous moment right at the very end. He had no idea she was in Aldeburgh in the first place – they both know she never contacts the family any more, and at first he hadn't recognized her, this screaming woman with her tangled hair and contorted face, crying out the composer's name. It was the voice that gave her away, and the way she was wringing her hands. Even then it was almost impossible to believe what he was seeing.

He had to leave his wife while he rushed out to try and help, to explain who he was before being led round to a side room. When the locked door was opened he found himself confronted by an hysterical wreck, still weeping and sobbing, still lashing out, to all intents and purposes a stranger who accused him of spying on her, of being one of the enemies, who had to be physically manhandled off the premises.

He and his wife stayed with her, he continues, until the taxi dropped them off at the address where she was staying. They tried to calm her. She'd obviously had far too much to drink; she reeked of brandy. They didn't leave for the drive home until they were satisfied she was ready for bed. They are both bone-tired.

Together they review the bouts of depression, the wayward job history, and the family's shared but unspoken consensus that out of sight had become out of mind. She was, in any case, an adult with a career and a life of her own. Her admiration for the composer had been treated as a harmless albeit eccentric hobby. They never realised the situation had become so grave.

He'd got up at the crack of dawn, the brother continues, and driven back to the Aldeburgh boarding house to check on her safety and wellbeing. Over breakfast in a nearby café he'd remonstrated with her, pleaded with her to come to her senses, said that she must never, ever do this again. What on earth was she thinking of? But there seemed to be no connection. Her eyes were blank and she refused to meet his gaze. She pleaded a splitting headache and said she was too exhausted to talk before promising to mend her behaviour. He'd left in deep disquiet, feeling helpless, but what more could he do? His sister agrees – what more indeed. The hall has his telephone number.

His misgivings turn out to have been well founded. She may have given him the assurances he was seeking but no one can begin to comprehend the depths of the compulsion that drives her to invade the hall again the next day, even though the stage door has been locked this time as a precaution. She enters undetected by the front door instead as Britten and Pears are mid-recital, and Britten is forced once more to escape through a different door.

And it is all repeated on the third night of the Festival when the opera is staged again. But this time the police are ready. The decision is made. Her family agree they have no choice but to commit her to an institution where she will spend the next six months, getting the psychiatric care she so desperately needs,

Urged on by Pears and by Duncan, Britten agrees he needs legal assistance. The woman's family may have assumed responsibility for her, but the stress is insupportable. He has learned that she will be released from the institution soon because the long weeks of treatment have been completed. It's been deemed a success. In all other respects the doctors and psychiatrists say she is essentially a rational woman who gives every impression of accepting that her behaviour was a delusional aberration. Provided she continues to be monitored and takes the prescribed medication, all should be well.

But Britten is not so sure. He has just returned from a trip abroad and can no longer ignore the recent past or hide from its implications. He still feels vulnerable. The sound of her dreadful cries continues to torment his sleep, and the doctors' professional assurances have not removed the residual anxieties about what could happen to her in the future. Most of all, the family's lack of any forward plan for the woman is especially troubling. It is time for an intervention, time to consult his lawyer and long-standing friend, Isador Caplan.

The two men meet in Caplan's London office and explore the options. Caplan is an ardent admirer and champion of Britten's music, and one of the Festival's co-founders. He enjoys a reputation as a skilled and persistent negotiator. The decision they jointly arrive at may appear extreme, but there are many precedents for sending problem family members to the colonies, dating from the remittance men of the nineteenth century and beyond. Besides, the institutions in the Old Commonwealth countries mirror those of the mother country, and most compelling of all, they offer acceptable simulacra of English ways and society. What could be better than a new start in a new country, New Zealand, for this sad woman, so she can put her obsession behind her once and for all.

A necessary conviction that this is prompted by altruism makes the proposed course of action all the more acceptable. They agree that any correspondence will be handled by Caplan alone, and that it will remain absolutely confidential. The family will be consulted about the offer, but Caplan is confident the terms will be accepted. After all, it will be as much to the family's advantage as theirs. A troublesome relative will have her passage paid for, and a teaching post will be found for her to take up on arrival.

The lawyer and his client shake hands and Britten is driven away in the black Rolls Royce waiting for him on the street outside. Nonetheless he cannot escape the nagging sense that this is a self-serving solution involving the egregious manipulation of another person's life, and for a moment he suffers a genuine pang of conscience.

Then he remembers what is in the balance – his peace of mind, or hers. This solution seems an answer to both.

CHAPTER 14

1955, Out of Sight

The doctors have said she is better and that the therapy and the drugs have worked. They smile encouragingly. It is time for her to return to her life, they say, and to use her talents.

The brother and sister hold another family council before they collect her, and the parents accept the invitation to meet the composer's lawyer in his London office – all expenses paid. Unnerved by Caplan's tall good looks, by his authority and his charm and by the imposing Mayfair address, they feel provincial, ill at ease, out of their depth. He tells them he has had extensive discussions with his client. The way forward is outlined and presumptively agreed. The offer of help and financial support prove decisive.

Far from blaming her, the lawyer stresses, his client pities their daughter who is all too clearly a victim of her delusions. He bears no ill will or rancour.

He only wants the best for her and to help her if he can. But she is also a threat to his peace of mind that he cannot entertain or afford. The constant sense of dread and anxiety is insupportable; it is having a damaging impact on his professional life. That is why the lawyer will help the family make arrangements for her to leave the country. The proposal is explained, kindly but firmly, and the plan takes shape.

While she was in hospital her family had already searched through the magazines that advertise teaching posts, including posts abroad, so the lawyer's suggestions are well timed, chiming as they do with their own tentative explorations. Besides, New Zealand is far away, far from memories, far from the object of her obsession. The lawyer adds that the composer is prepared to use his influence to help her find a suitable position in a private girls' school. He has contacts. The offer is welcomed, but there is one binding condition. The lawyer is adamant. No one must ever know about this except the people present in the room.

They have told me what has been decided – decided behind my back as if I am nothing, a nobody. As if I do not count. They never consulted me about anything.

How dare they. But on the other hand, I can see why not, because what is left of my life without Ben? They even said it is true about him and Peter Pears, but I still refuse to believe it. It is illegal for one thing, and if it was true why would he have sent me all those messages, the messages that said he loved me, that we were destined to be together.

They have always felt I am a nuisance, a nobody. When they said they were going to send me to New Zealand they tried to make it sound like a wonderful opportunity. It's supposed to be a beautiful country they said, full of mountains, beaches, lakes, flightless birds, no snakes. As if I cared. I don't know why they think any of that would appeal to me. How could it. Besides, how will Ben contact me when I am so far away. How can I betray his love by leaving him like this, by abandoning him.

I only agreed when they told me it was Ben's idea, and that he is going to help find me a job there as a teacher. So he still cares. He loves me after all, because why else would he go to so much trouble for me. I understand everything again – he is sending me another message. He has never stopped thinking about me.

I will go there for a while until my actions at the Festival, at the opera, are forgiven and forgotten, because they have told me repeatedly that I did in fact shock him deeply. He has immaculate manners, and I'm prepared to accept that I did breach them utterly, but I couldn't help it. Yes, it was a moment of madness, a week of madness in fact, but I can see that now and I'm feeling much better. It is time for me to make the sacrifice he is asking of me so that one day we can be together again.

And I can still send him postcards and letters so that he knows I am safe, still faithful to our past and our future.

Until then it will stay our secret because his lawyer says Ben doesn't want me to talk about what happened yet. Or ever. One day he will tell me why. At present I will submit to his wishes and keep our secret because he has asked me to do so. Because I know he still needs me, and always will.

Meanwhile the nightmares have returned. I told the doctors they had gone but it's not true. I dread going to bed. It is the same every time – I am back at Crag House, in his bedroom, watching him sleeping. Then I see that another person is in bed beside him. The blankets heave as the two bodies start writhing together, moving up and down in unison, absorbed in each other, panting and grunting. The person on top starts to pound the other, his buttocks heaving, faster and faster. Then shockingly, he turns around and looks at me mockingly before resuming his filthy act. His face is the face of Peter Pears. The man pinned beneath him is Ben, my Ben.

I am transfixed, frozen to the spot. In the worst nightmares of all his legs and thighs begin to sprout great coarse tufts of hair, like a satyr's, and he beckons to me obscenely, inviting me to join them.

Chapter 14

Full Circle

The girls' school is in the suburbs of a small seaport town. The pupils are mostly boarders from tough sheep-farming families, some from high country stations where great shingle screes turn the steep slopes grey and snow-fed rivers snake their way down to the sea in ribbons of milky-blue channels, some broad and deep, others mere streams, glistening between the boulder beds that sprawl across the valleys.

The school claims a reputation for its music. There the teacher can continue her recovery and make a new life. The family are relieved when she appears to acquiesce. Besides, why raise doubts when everything seems to be going so smoothly. It is easier, and infinitely more convenient, to accept her agreement at face value. But what they fail to realise, or refuse to consider, is that inside she is secretly hugging to herself the inviolate knowledge that she is still Ben's wife, and that this will sustain her wherever she goes.

For what do they know about being 'better'. Or about the ECT treatments that left her exhausted, her brain dulled and her limbs aching from the convulsions, the drugs that left her unable to get out of bed in the mornings. Her passion is her lifeline, her very reason for existing. Her love cannot be extinguished with pills and therapy. It is too strong, too transcendent. Without it she is nothing. Like the devouts she has read about, the women who shave their heads and become brides of Christ, who commit themselves to a life of seclusion and prayer, she shares the same sense of a holy calling and a sacred commitment. To Ben. Her Ben. Her light, her love, her husband, her life.

She will need all the sustenance she can muster, and over the months to come this knowledge will be her anchor. She is about to set sail on an ocean liner that will take her to a small country on the other side of the world. Its nearest land mass is Antarctica. The vast neighbouring continent of Australia lies 3000 miles away across the Tasman Sea. When the boat stops at different ports on the way, Palma, Naples, Bombay, Cairo, Aden, Singapore, Manila, Sydney, instead of joining the shore-bound groups of sightseers she stays behind on board so she can nurse her bereavement and keep it alive. Other passengers include families on the Assisted Migration Scheme – the Ten Pound Poms. She has no desire to mingle with them at all.

She learns that the town she is going to has one cinema, one theatre, a hall with a sound shell sitting on the bay, and in summer a giant seaside ferris wheel. The water in the harbour is notorious for the untreated sewage reputed to float in on the tides.

On the outskirts is a large abattoir where the sheep that make up the country's principal export are slaughtered by the thousand and their flayed carcasses frozen and shipped back to England. When the wind blows from the west the foul smell of incinerated waste blankets the air for miles around. Inland, the foothills of the Southern Alps lie draped across their undulating horizons, shielding the plains from the snow-capped mountains beyond. The South Island winters are notoriously harsh; during the coldest months frost routinely attaches itself to the insides of dormitory windows. Chilblains torment cracked swollen fingers. Influenza is endemic.

After London, even Huddersfield, her new home will feel like a cultural desert. Access to the concerts she used to go to, and opportunities for travel, will be unbearably limited. She will have to live in a dispiriting brick and pebble-dash bungalow in a corner of the school grounds alongside other members of the school's staff, women she has never met, and share their lives. She already knows common ground will be non-existent. It will also be coruscatingly lonely. Yet this is where she is expected to start afresh and to continue her fragile path to recovery, a path she is unable to embrace because that will mean the death of her dream, and the end of the dream will mean the death of herself.

For the teacher it is the girl that makes the difference. The girl with the titian hair who seems to live in a world of her own, who reminds her of herself. The teacher needs someone to confide in, someone who will become an unknowing, but essential ally. Someone she can use to assuage her loneliness. At times this is almost insupportable. The girl is her lifeline. The stranger on the train.

The school's head mistress is new, like me, and also from England. She greeted me with distant courtesy when we met, a small plain woman with no make-up, mousey hair, and a shiny nose. Her cheeks are blotched red with rosacea. She wears dowdy clothes and ugly lace-up shoes, and swallows her words in a way common to English women of her age and class, but she seems far too unworldly for the role she finds herself in. I suspect there's a connection somewhere, that she's part of the reason I have this job. An invisible elderly mother apparently shares their separate flat in the seniors' boarding house, next door to the sanatorium.

They say she tried to remove the wrinkles from her first pair of nylon stockings with a hot iron before setting off for Sunday church, and had to appear in old lisle stockings instead. She has already become an object of ridicule. Her presence here is even more inexplicable than my own.

It is as bad as I had feared. The endless uniforms, the ugly dark green tunics the girls wear, the ties with their ugly green and blue stripes, the ugly accents. I have never felt more of an outsider in my life. The six other teachers here in the equally ugly staff house all seem to know each other, but none of them seem to like each other. And they certainly don't like me. All I can say is it's mutual. I avoid getting involved in their petty jealousies and gossip. Instead I keep myself to myself, just as I always have. It is like being locked in a perpetual staff room for 24 hours a day with no way out.

I also have to share the staff house kitchen with its mean little cupboards labelled with our individual names, or sit at the staff table in the school's dining hall, watched by a hundred pairs of eyes, forced to eat the same kind of food I had to eat in the hospital – endless white bread and pink jam from huge catering tins, filled out with turnip pulp and sawdust instead of raspberry seeds. I know this because another teacher told me so. I can believe her. Egg powder is used for scrambled egg here too, just like in England. It's like eating pus. I fail to understand why. This is a land of farmers. I've never seen more room to keep hens. And why no sign of the Maoris, the native New Zealanders? I've been told they came here first but they seem invisible. The same teacher was airily dismissive when I asked her about this, saying they all live in the North Island.

I know they despise me, and if they pretend otherwise I can see through them. There is no humanity, no compassion, no sensibility. They think I'm weak, pathetic.

I can tell, because I've been treated like that in the past – by my family and by colleagues. It is Ben's love that sustains me, a love no one else can begin to understand because I was, and always will be, the person he chose. I write to him every week and think of him every hour. One day I'll post the letters. When he realises how lonely I am

I know he will bring me back to England. It is just a matter of waiting, and of being patient – endlessly patient.

As for the teaching facilities, I have to make do with an ugly little hut at the end of a row of other ugly little huts, and a piano that is not even properly tuned. I've done my best, putting up postcards on the wall and other pictures to remind me of everything I hold dear. Without them I think I'd go mad, or maybe I should say madder. After all, that's what my family said I was.

If I couldn't make myself angry I'd never stop crying. When I remember to take the pills it's better, but I keep on forgetting, and then I don't know whether to cry or laugh. I feel as if the pills are blunting my senses, and sometimes I find myself watching myself as if from a distance, wondering where I've disappeared to, who I really am.

If it weren't for the girl I would have gone mad already. When she walked through the door for that first piano lesson, I saw straightaway that she is different. She seems aware of a life beyond the school, she asks questions about other places, other countries, and she seems hungry for more. She knows about opera, she has plans for her future.

She has quite simply transfixed me, and she listens when I talk about Ben. She really listens. I cannot describe the relief I feel – to have someone to talk to about him, someone I can teach to play, the way he does.

She is a reserved child, watchful, cautious even, but that is something I can identify with, because I was a reserved child myself. And her extraordinary red hair is the most beautiful titian colour. I can sense she hates me talking about it because girls her age are always self-conscious, but one day she will realise what a gift it is. The colour is matched by her brown eyes, the same colouring Rossetti loved to paint, the same colouring as Lizzie Siddal.

Right now she is like raw material; I will awaken her, try and mould her, and show her the kind of life she can aspire to, a life of the arts, travel, music, and above all Ben's music. Without her I would find it all intolerable. The other girls are like barbarians. They have no interest in culture, in beauty or aesthetics. They are an army of feral monsters incapable of listening, or learning. They make teaching impossible. I can sense them conspiring against me and I want to scream at them when they whisper and fidget. Instead I keep my dignity because I am better than them, and Ben loves me.

The girl is my protection and my ally.

The classes continue, but their tenor changes. The girl sits passively, listening to the teacher's tales of Britten and her journeys in his wake, to the accounts of recitals and operas. When the teacher pauses she asks her to carry on. The teacher scents victory and the lessons become centred more and more round her recollections. In between, the trite piano pieces the girl has brought to the lessons in her satchel give way to Dubussy and Ravel, and to exercises designed to train the child's hands and lay the foundations for the technical skills that will enable her talent to develop and flourish, exercises based on Britten's technique, a technique the teacher has herself diligently mastered both as homage and gift.

The teacher starts to see the girl as a mirror of herself at the same age, with the same reserve and resistance, but in essence she is too absorbed by her own misery to realise how abusive this is. Her wish for a reflection of herself blinds her to the truth – that she is once again turning an unconsenting third party into the unwanted recipient of her own delusions. It is a toxic process of transference that fails to recognize the girl's own autonomy and capacity for repudiation.

The strategy is fatally flawed from the outset. The emotional prop the teacher constructs is as deceptive as her illusions and the girl is protected by a powerful sense of self-preservation. There was always going to be the day of reckoning and so it proves. The Judas day.

*

I would like to be able to write a reassuring coda, to say I eventually discovered she returned to England where her obsession gently withered as further treatment and a loving family's support restored her to mental and physical health. But I cannot, because I do not know what happened, and like so much else I never will. It is all conjecture in any case, a blend of fact and fiction based on circumstantial evidence and gut instinct only.

Maybe she became worse and ended up locked in some institution, still believing that her Ben loved her. Maybe she slipped away and died of grief, or became another suicide statistic. Maybe she found another teaching post, fell in love, married, and lived happily ever after – the least likely scenario of all I'm afraid. Was she still listening to his works and still detecting messages when he wrote *Phaedre* twenty years later, with its anguished reiterations of 'I Love you, I love you.'[16]

Whatever the case I have squared the circle as far as possible, and in the final analysis am left feeling infinitely sorry for a woman who was victim of a cruel pathology she was unable to control.

But wait. I owe this woman more. I've invested too much of myself in her to let her go, tested my powers of invention to bridge the gaps, sometimes to their limit. I'm not prepared, or able, to abandon her so easily. She deserves a future – so let's construct one.

STALKER: WALL OF SILENCE

Part 2

CHAPTER 16

Into beyond

In fact none of these things happen to her. None of them at all.

Julia Verne doesn't get married, and she doesn't become any sicker than she was. This is a woman who is still capable of surprises, and whose humiliation fuels an anger so deep that it also fuels her future in ways she never dreamed of.

Back in the staff house kitchen she wipes the tears from her eyes and blows the snot from her nose before opening the knife drawer, choosing one that's as narrow and pointed as a stiletto. A faint odour of fish clings to the handle. She is alone – all the other teachers are still busy taking their classes in the main building. She slides her finger along the edge of the smooth steel blade, up and down, picturing the blood dripping from her wrists, pooling on the floor, clotting in the corners after she has collapsed, the missed splashes on the skirting boards, a faceless cleaning woman on her knees, attacking the rust-coloured stains with a scrubbing brush.

But the thought of the satisfaction her actions may give, of the faux horror of colleagues she has come to despise, the one with the face like a hatchet and the empty smile, makes her pause. She notes how blunt the knife is, wonders why no one has thought to sharpen it, where the sharpener is hidden, then replaces it and slams the drawer shut. She has to get away, immediately, anywhere but the school after four months of hell. The thought of strangers clearing her abandoned room, taking the postcards down from the walls, throwing her clothes carelessly into a refuse bag, consigning her to oblivion, feeds her anger, the hurt and humiliation, still further.

The glass she hurls at one of the cabinets explodes on impact with a crash, shattering into a thousand shards. The pieces lie glittering on the ground in a shaft of sunlight that splits the floor in two. She's never thrown a glass in anger before; in films broken glasses and broken bottles smashed over a rival's head are harmless theatre, made of sugar and cleared away by stage hands, but this is real life, not pretend.

For the girl's rejection has been an awakening, a realisation of how false all her fantasies have been, how her life has been built on an illusion. Like an alcoholic she has hit rock bottom: the only way from now on is forward. Onwards and upwards. The anger is redirected at the obsession that has framed her identity, that has taken over her life. For the first time she sees herself as others have and understands why the other women avoided her, why her pupils never warmed to her or respected her. Why should they? A person without a core, a construct without a soul. They were right, she was wrong. Time to find out who she really is.

She finishes packing, flinging a few clothes into the one suitcase, abandoning the rest, the filmy scarves and floating dresses, tearing down the postcards, ripping up the old programmes, and calls for a taxi. When the driver asks her where she's going she tells him to drop her off at the bus station, but it's late in the day by the time she gets there. The light is fading and the last buses have left. She ends up spending the night at a nearby hotel in a barren room that smells of cigarettes and despair. She's the only woman on her own there, and woefully out of place in her calf-length dress and apricot cardigan. Looking in the mirror, she makes a decision and takes her nail scissors out of her bag, hacking at her hair until it's short all over and the jagged tufts have been tamed until it looks more like a style, less a cry for help. Clumps and clumps drop onto the chest of drawers in front of her. The new face is almost unrecognisable – younger, with the features accentuated, the bone structure sharpened. The old maid look has disappeared. For the next few months, whenever she sees herself reflected in a mirror or shop window she will wonder who the stranger is looking back at her. The following morning she makes a quick visit to the town's main street and buys trousers, shirts, socks, walking shoes, a couple of pullovers and an anorak before dumping the dress and cardigan in the rubbish bin along with shorn clumps of hair from the night before.

She catches the first bus leaving. It's headed for Mount Cook, the mountain she's heard so much about. Aoraki, the cloud piercer. It could have been a bus to anywhere; the timing dictates her destination. A random decision, trusting to fate.

The journey inland, over the pass and down into the Mackenzie country beyond, makes her feel like a tourist for the first time since her arrival, an outcast no longer. She forces her hands to stay still, to stop compulsively twisting and turning in her lap. But what will she do when she arrives? She's heard about the famous lodge, the Mt Cook Hermitage. She will see if she can get a job there, any job, even as a cleaner. Anything that distances her from the memories and the misery of the past few months.

The headmistress gets her letter of resignation a fortnight later and the police take her off their missing persons register.

When the huge sprawling vista the other side of the pass opens out before her she has to fight off an attack of almost suffocating agoraphobia. The sweeping tussock-covered land, the pale wintered willow trees that line the winding rivers, and the mountain ranges disappearing into the distance, make her want to shut her eyes, block it all out, retreat back inside herself.

But anything has to be better than the school's claustrophobic hothouse atmosphere and the dingy staff house with its south-facing kitchen, dark and shadowed in an upside down world where even the water goes down plugholes in reverse. She clasps her hands together again, clenching and unclenching them, bracing herself for the unknown.

The driver informs the passengers that the crystalline aquamarine of the lake the bus is rumbling past owes its startling colour to particles of glacial sediment that refract the sun's rays. The long journey up the dusty shingle road, its dirt surface corrugated like a washboard, is a bone-shaking reminder that she is in a new country with a transport infrastructure that is still a work in progress. Flattened carcasses punctuate the miles – run-over rabbits, hares and possums. Hedgehogs too, prickles pointing skyward like toothpicks. Hawks tear at entrails expelled from crushed bodies and lumber into the air as the bus bears down on them, just in time to avoid being crushed in turn.

When the bus stops at the half-way point she moves to a seat nearer the front, feeling nauseous after the road's twists and turns, and the hairpin bends. On the way she had glimpsed the rusted belly of an overturned lorry in a gully hundreds of feet below, partly hidden by gorse, the same gorse that grows in Scotland but here a ravenous invader that has spread out of control, smothering hillsides and making grazing impossible. Everything is different: she wonders why she is only now discovering this, why she had allowed the school to become a prison so quickly.

With her hands she touches her newly short hair again, already coated with the dust churned up by the bus's wheels. Few people would recognize her now in the new casual clothes and shorter hairstyle, and that is what she wants – to start anew, anonymous, safe from being discovered and being forcibly returned to the school, the pills, or England.

The other passengers are mostly younger, fresh-faced,

bright-eyed, armed with tramping boots and backpacks, looking forward to the trails in the national park. Maybe she will join them? Try tramping herself. Forget she was a music teacher. Forget about the school. Forget about Ben, about the asylum. Forget about everything.

The mountain slowly emerges into view at the head of the lake, small at first, looming larger and larger as the bus eats up the miles. The white clouds obscuring the peak suddenly clear, whipped away as if by magic. Gusts of wind-blown snow scud the air. She imagines looking through binoculars, spying miniscule figures trudging along a ridge before being lost in clouds that reappear as quickly as they vanish. Two climbers had fallen to their deaths only a week beforehand when the weather descended, treacherously. It took three days before their bodies were found, still roped together, the one dragged to his death by the other's moment of carelessness, or misstep, or failure to dig in his ice axe. Or a loose crampon. No one will ever know.

By the time the bus pulls up at the lodge she is thirsty and tired, and her hair fees stiff and brittle-dry. The other passengers go off to register for their bookings in the huts and camp grounds. Windbreaks of manuka and sharp-thorned matagouri screen a gravel path leading to the entrance. Giant snow tussocks billow in the wintery breeze blowing down the valley. More affluent visitors who have come by car book into the lodge itself. At the front desk she is asked for her name and whether she has reserved a room, whether she is on her own or with her husband.

Neither, she replies. She's from England. She's looking for work and on an impulse has come up to Mt Cook to see if there is anything available here. Any job, she repeats, any job at all. She's worked as a cleaner, in restaurants, even in the kitchens. She's making it up as she goes along, reading the receptionist's watchful face for any flicker that tells her she's on the right track. The woman frowns, then tells her to wait while she dials a number on the in-house phone. It's early June, the off season, coming up to mid-winter when buildings are rimed with frost in the mornings and snow blankets the ground. Visitor numbers are down.

Her spirits sag, and she wonders why she has been so foolishly impulsive. A wave of exhaustion overcomes her and she turns to go, defeated already.

But the receptionist replaces the phone with a look of surprise on her face. 'You're in luck,' she says, 'although it's a job you may not want. And it's only temporary too – one of our staff has had to leave, at short notice too. It's left us in a bit of a bind. We need an extra body on housekeeping.'

In the staff annexe she unpacks her case, hanging the new clothes in the cupboard between the two beds in the room she will be sharing, putting them away in the allocated drawers. She reminds herself that she is still young. Time to shake off the middle-aged habits she has saddled herself with, to make up for the wasted years.

Her new roommate is Luisa from Chile. They are put on bedroom duty together the next morning, changing sheets, emptying wastepaper baskets, polishing taps, so the first conversations are about changing sheets, emptying bins, and polishing taps, before topics are broadened to include Luisa's impressions of the country and what she thinks. 'It's a good job here,' Luisa tells Julia, 'not difficult, good food too.'

Luisa has long blond hair tied back for work, the rest of the time hanging loose. The Spanish accent makes her husky English sound exotic, and sometimes incomprehensible. Luisa wants to speak better English before she returns to Chile to become a language teacher. She has a lot of work to do. Julia wonders what the flat New Zealand accent, with the question marks that interrogate the end of every sentence, will sound like when grafted onto Luisa's sibilant s's and her insistence on treating g's as h's. As the weeks pass and the two women settle into each other's company, Julia offers to help Luisa with conversation sessions, tactfully pointing out that her own accent is 'English' English, not American or New Zealand English, and therefore by definition the correct one.

Julia notes Luisa's wardrobe carefully, sees how it lightens up her youth. The bright colours Luisa wears set off her deep brown eyes and tanned skin; the blond ponytail swings from side to side like a tassel. As they change beds together, piling the used laundry into big bins on wheels, dust surfaces and sweep and polish corridors, Julia learns about Chile and about Luisa's home in Santiago, where her boyfriend Jorge is waiting for her. They met as students and plan to get married, but Jorge's mother is a problem because she is extremely possessive. Jorge is her only son. She wants him to live at home until he's thirty.

Jorge loves her deeply, Luisa says, '*El me ama mucho.*' And she loves him back, '*Me encanta.*' Luisa conveys in inventive sign language that she is no longer a virgin, but a woman of experience, and Julia adopts a worldly air, embarrassed by her own lack of experience and Luisa's assumptions. Virginity for Luisa is not a virtue but a rite-of-passage milestone she and Jorge have navigated together, mindful of unwanted consequences, sealing a mutual commitment before Luisa's travels. Luisa's vocabulary expands in surprising ways as she looks for the words to impart her secrets, because secrets are never so safe as when told to a stranger, and this awkward roommate who wears her clothes as if they are a disguise is definitely a stranger.

Luisa is also still young enough to be entirely self-obsessed and self-referential. She will never ask Julia for reciprocal confidences, and indeed scarcely asks her any questions about herself at all. And for Julia that's just the way she wants it. Untroubled by modesty, Luisa dresses and undresses her young body with its smooth creamy skin as if she were Eve before the serpent. Julia can see why Luisa and Jorge's mother are already at loggerheads.

I have a new job, the kind of job I've never dreamt of doing. Call it good luck, or fate. I'm not sure which.

I'm working as a cleaning lady, or chambermaid, or cleaner, I'm actually not sure what it's called, at The Hermitage up by Mt Cook, New Zealand's highest mountain. It all feels like an accident. If anyone had told me a week ago that this is what I'd be doing I'd never have believed them. So much for the impossible. It's the opposite of what I was doing. For one thing it's up in the mountains, not by the seaside, and I'm making beds and cleaning bathrooms, not teaching music. Also there are no schoolgirls, no school, no responsibility. No one to betray me. I cannot express the peace I feel. A weight has been lifted off my shoulders and I feel dizzy with relief.

I've never done anything like this before, I suppose because I never thought it was possible to change my life on the spur of the moment and walk away from it, just like that. All the bad things suddenly seem distant and irrelevant, and utterly meaningless. I have to ask myself why it took me so long, why I have wasted years and years living a life I hated. Why have I been such a fool.

It's as if I have been blind all along and have had my sight restored. The mountain changes every day. Sometimes I can't even see it for the cloud and the rain.

At other times it's as clear as clear can be, and bathed in dazzling sunshine. It dominates everything with its size and power. But it's also dangerous and has claimed many lives. It's where Edmund Hillary trained before conquering Everest – the same day as the Queen's Coronation. That seems much longer ago than three years. I never thought I'd one day be working in its shadow. I'm starting to feel that everything has turned out for the best after all. If a mountain can change from day to day, so can I.

I'd thought my life was over. It seems it's only just beginning

*

The Venice trip seems a timid excursion by comparison with Luisa's bold sense of adventure. The cheerful confidence of the occasional trampers she meets on her days off and their sunny enthusiasm is contagious. She buys more clothes, warmer ones, and hikes up a steep bush track leading to the peat tarns nestled in the hills above the lodge, pausing at intervals to catch her breath and listen to the crack and rumble of distant avalanches, watching out for tell-tale plumes of snow. At the foot of the glacier snaking down the mountain, noisy meltwater rushes beneath the dirty ice on its way to the head of the lake. An underworld Styx. Orpheus waiting for Charon. Ceberus and Eurydice.

As she returns the greetings on the tracks, the holas and hellos, Julia is already feeling part of a wider, kinder community and Luisa's English is improving exponentially. As winter morphs into spring, then summer, she carries on moving forward, determined to make up for all the lost years when she was a pale imitation of what she could be. Wondering how and why had she ever consented to a lifestyle that ended up circumscribing almost everything she did?

It is all going well until the day she passes someone in the corridor on a Saturday morning, a guest, someone whose face is familiar. Disturbingly so. The fleeting encounter leaves her feeling sick with apprehension. With an effort she digs deep into suppressed memory and locates the face. It belongs to one of the teachers from the school.

Her first impulse is to turn around, to pack her case and run, anywhere but here. She vomits into a basin, gripping the sides to prevent her knees buckling beneath her, then runs a tap and sits down, beads of sweat glistening on her forehead, before taking a deep breath as the panic attack subsides, forcing herself to pause and regroup. Luisa comes up looking concerned, asking what the matter is. The girl's gentle touch on her arm calms her and her breathing returns to normal, restored by the solicitude. 'Nothing,' she replies, 'just a moment of dizziness. I'm fine now.' And so she is. Hatchet Face hadn't recognized her in her cleaner's uniform, proof that it's made her invisible, her role as a chambermaid even more so. The encounter was a fluke, the disguise worked. It won't happen again and besides, now she is forewarned, forearmed.

The sight every day of the mountain, looming majestically above, sometimes illuminated by bright sunshine that turns its snow-clad flanks into sheets of glittering incandescence, at other times hidden by the sudden clouds that sweep up from the island's western flank, lifts and dashes her spirits in equal measure. The determination of the steady procession of climbers descending from its peak is a reminder that success has to be earned if it is to be won. Their blackened finger tips and scabbed, wind-scarred features seem to do little to blunt their enthusiasm or their stubborn belief that whatever the cost, the effort is worth it.

When the manuka bursts into spring-time bloom, the myriad small white and pink-flushed flowers fill the air with a musky fragrance, and the bees descend en masse to collect the sweet nectar.

1st January, 1957. This is the strangest Christmas I've ever had – roast turkey in the middle of summer complete with roast potatoes and stuffing, strings of Christmas cards showing robin redbreasts, even though most people here have never even seen a robin, and bunches of holly with bright red berries in scenes of snow-covered villages and carol singers. Cotton-wool snowflakes are still glued to the lodge's windows, just like in England even though it's summer here, and last night, New Year's Eve, we all stayed up until midnight and sang Auld Lang Syne together. I know New Zealand is a new country, but just how new I hadn't fully appreciated until now. Naturally it made me feel a little bit homesick. But then I remembered how cold and empty the old Christmases with my parents were, and the way I always felt left out, how there never seemed to be any real affection, as if I was there on sufferance only. Looking back I can see how much I hated those Christmases, and the embarrassment of opening presents I never wanted but had to pretend to like out of politeness. My parents were pretending too, pretending that I was welcome when we all knew I was only there because they felt duty bound to invite me, not because they wanted me.

Here there's a camaraderie amongst us workers that I've never experienced before, never with my family, and certainly not in the staff rooms from my teaching days. Here we all feel equal. Everyone joins in together, and I'm feeling stronger and healthier than I've ever been. I'm going into the nearest town later this week to buy summer clothes because it's suddenly become hot, and it's going to become even hotter. So I'll need to get sunglasses too. The light here is different to the light in England. It's brighter, harsher, more glaring. Everything seems more vivid, more alive.

CHAPTER 17

The Coast

The holiday season with its barrage of alpine visitors has come and gone, and Luisa is leaving to go fruit picking down south, amongst the stoned fruit orchards – cherries, nectarines, apricots. Jorge is coming over to join her before they return home together. Julia takes stock and decides to move on too. Julia has no desire to get used to Luisa's replacement. Besides, she's been here long enough. She no longer needs a sanctuary. High time to move and see more of this country while she can.

But where to next? That's the problem with choice, as Julia is discovering. Or should she let choice choose her? A group are taking a minibus to the West Coast and there's a spare seat. Serendipity, carpe diem. She's learned that the Coast has a reputation for being the outlier province, backward, isolated, cut off from the rest of the country, proud of its exceptionalism. The West Coaster myth – rough, tough, and self-sufficient. It's also a place where people go to hide, and Julia is still in hiding, from her former self and from any encounter with her previous life. She is now sleeping soundly, and the physical work has made her tougher mentally as well, ready for early bedtimes. She no longer dreads insomnia or the dreams that used to make her wake up gasping in horror, drenched in sweat and night terrors. But she remains aware of her parlous fragility. One step at a time.

The minibus heads off for Westport, once a hectic mining town way back in the 1860s. The nearest headland, Cape Foulwind, testifies to its climate. A big bearded man in a plaid shirt and stained khaki shorts plumps himself down on the seat next to hers. Thick woollen socks peek over the tops of enormous boots. His muscled arms are coated with a fuzz of golden hairs and the bridge of his nose is flattened to one side. The bear says his name is Barry. On impulse she replies that she's Veronica, as good a time as any to make up another name, and he accepts it without question. Veronica. She never knew it could be so easy to become some one else and puts it down to Luisa's easy acceptance of each day as it comes and the blessings of anonymity. And to her new look, the short hairstyle that matches her age, not her mother's, the hiking trousers that suit her slim hips and long legs. She's relieved she's replaced the suitcase with a rucksack, like the other travellers. It makes her more nimble, better able to travel spontaneously. Carrying her house with her like a snail or hermit crab.

It's another long drive along the ubiquitous shingle roads, and takes a whole day. Something is wrong with the suspension; there's a long break while a flat tyre is replaced; the engine needs a top-up of oil; it overheats on the hills. More dust clings to her, but her hair is better cut now, less inclined to stick up in the wrong places. Luisa had sorted it out before she left, deftly snipping away, standing back to admire her handiwork.

Much of the journey feels like retracing her steps but hours later the minibus is over the top of another pass and they are deep in bush country, hedged in by dense vegetation that looks to her untrained eye like a jungle, the tall tree ferns with their crowns like outsized umbrellas as exotic as peacocks. Barry is a West Coaster and when he finds out she's never been to the Coast before she discovers he's a talker as well. A fair number of people, including ill-prepared walkers, disappear into the bush never to be seen again he says. It only takes a few steps before all sense of location is lost, 'And then you're a goner'. In abandoned settlements lonely crosses mark the anonymous graves of miners and wanderers, dreamers seeking their fortunes, men and women lost to disease, weather, sickness, accidents, murder.

He's been doing some deer culling for the government, Barry adds. Getting a few possums on the side too, for the bounty. And whitebaiting. He has digs in Westport, and asks where she's staying. He tells her the name of a boarding house with cheap rates.

'You'll make some mates there,' he says, 'find someone to explore the Coast with. You're a Pom, aren't you? Tell you what, I'll show you round the town, take you to the pub. How about tomorrow night, after we've slept off today. It's going to be a long one.'

Barry's right. It takes more than eight hours before the minibus ends its journey and drops the passengers off, stiff and weary after sitting for so long, with only a few breaks to stretch their legs and buy pies and drinks from cafes and milk bars with boards advertising ice cream. From time to time Barry falls asleep, his head slipping sideways by degrees until it's resting on her shoulder, more bison than bear she thinks, giving him a discreet nudge. It's curiously intimate. What would Luisa say?

When he awakes he shakes his head like a dog getting out of a lake and yawns before apologising. 'Yeah, tomorrow night,' he repeats. Right now he's knackered. 'I'll drop by around 6 and pick you up? OK?'

'But what about the 6 o'clock closing time? The six-o'clock swill?'

'Nah, no worries,' Barry replies. 'It's all a bit different on the coast.'

Brief years of prosperity driven by the distant gold rush have left the West Coast with a legacy of abandoned hope and stubborn self-reliance. In Westport itself a few villas remain, embellished with curved verandas and decorative ironwork, weatherboarded witnesses to historic bursts of gold rush prosperity and indiscriminate tree felling, but otherwise the town feels sad, almost abandoned.

Thin wiry farmers who cannot afford to go anywhere else linger on, their faces pinched by poverty, ground down by the climate, unable to sell, unable to leave. Loners turn up with their swags and stay because they've reached the end of the road. Deer culling and milling sit alongside coal mines delivering up dirty lignite that will one day be shunned because of its toxicity. Whitebaiting, hunting and fishing attract sportsmen prepared to tolerate the stratospheric rainfalls and the swarms of ravenous sandflies. Nikau palms flourish along a stray length of sub-tropical microclimate. A giant snail the size of a fist with a glistening chestnut-brown shell presents a special hazard for trampers, and small native owls cry out at night for *more pork.* Other bird calls piercing as flutes mix with the whispering of the bush's rustling leaves, and all the while the roiling Tasman Sea picks up huge salt-bleached logs from river mouths and pulls them out to sea on vicious undertows before dumping them back on the long exposed coastline.

A truculent assertiveness is all that remains of the Coast's lost heyday. But the same assertiveness is already attracting a new breed of resident, refugees from 50s conformity, individualists who want to live freely, potters, artists, vegetarians. Within twenty years it will have become a haven for so-called alternative lifestyles and new age communes. What better place for her next sortie, for her next adventure.

She's sharing a room with two other women – sturdy young Germans with muscled calves and tans who ask her if she'd like to come with them and find a place to eat. Renate and Sigrid are touring the country having completed their degrees in modern languages. Next stop the Philippines. Unlike Luisa they are full of questions, as if a commitment to curiosity informs their every encounter. The new Veronica finds she is surprisingly creative when it comes to inventing answers and toys briefly with alternatives before saying she works in a UK government research institute and is currently on sabbatical leave. Strict confidentiality guidelines mean she cannot say more. Let's just say it's exciting and demanding. Or more often dull and routine. A break like this is what she's been needing.

Over fish and chips Renate and Sigrid compare the Southern Alps with Kitzbühel and the Interlaken, Mt Cook with the Matterhorn, London with Berlin. It's soon apparent that they are serious young women as the talk moves on to post-war Germany, post-war angst, and generational resentment. Why are they blamed for everything that happened in the war they ask reproachfully, when they were only children. OK, it was terrible, but it's not their fault.

But this is a subject that engages them more than it does her.

She remains silent because she has nothing to contribute. These new encounters are infinitely more therapeutic, she reflects, than all the pills put together. The composer, the school, opera, music, become more and more irrelevant with every passing day, and she has vowed to never wear apricot colours again. She's forgotten why she wore the colour in the first place – someone must have said it suited her, that it matched her hair, but she no longer recalls who it could have been. Bland, unassertive, neither orange nor gold. Somewhere in between. A nowhere colour without definition, a blur of mass and form stealing identity, leaving nothing except a void.

Meeting new people in random encounters linked by travel and chance: Julia has already discovered that each encounter merits attention in the moment only. Encounters with no backdrop and no future, encounters that allow her to move forward, unencumbered and debt free. Occasionally she will wonder what has happened to the people whose paths have crossed with hers, but only occasionally – Julia is by now committed to jettisoning baggage, not acquiring it.

She will never know, for instance, that Renate eventually moves with her husband and three children to Cologne, where she watches the flattened city slowly rise again in the course of an ambitious rebuilding programme. Her English helps her secure a job on the front desk of one of the art galleries the city becomes famous for. She struggles with her weight and becomes an early admirer of Gerhard Richter.

Or that Sigrid settles down in Munich and trains as a child psychologist. Or that the two German women will resume contact much later and start taking brief holidays together, rare escapes from their lives, returning to their families warmed and exhausted by the embraces they've shared, sweet stolen days when they relive who they were rather than what they have become, feeling each other's flesh, tasting each other's skin, tracing the faintly silvered stretch marks that lace their gently puckered bellies, shuddering with forgotten pleasures.

Westport is small, very small. She's seeing Barry later on, if he turns up. Otherwise there seems little to do apart from going to the glacier further down the coast. But no, it will take a whole day there and back. She'll explore the nearby beach instead, watch the pounding surf, wander amongst the great stacked piles of driftwood, envisage blue-tinted icebergs big as cathedrals floating far to the south, think of Scott and his team freezing to death in a tent scant miles from safety, of Shackleton listening to the groans of the *Endurance* as it splinters and cracks in the deadly embrace of the encircling floes, of the ancient mariner and an albatross's wingspan. The connections weave through her brain as she stumbles over pebbles and boulders and listens to the roar of the breakers pummelling the sloping foreshore, throwing up soaring plumes of salted spray. When I am old, she thinks, I will remember this.

Squeezed between the sea and bush-covered mountains, Westport can only be a place to pass through. She's heard of Nelson further north, its sunny climate, moderate rainfall, and relaxed lifestyle, of the golden sands and the Sounds with their hundreds of tiny bays fringed by native bush. Maybe a job in another national park? Or with one of the vineyards that are just starting to appear. Or fruit picking, like Luisa. But what after that? The old doubts are still rekindled easily. Let's see what Barry has to say. He's bound to have some suggestions. And remember to answer when he calls her Veronica.

Barry does turn up, on the dot of six, just as he had said. Julia glimpses the conscientious man behind the casual exterior. He's exchanged his shorts for trousers, and casually drapes his huge arm across her shoulders. She flinches at the unexpected contact, the smell of his sweat, then forces herself to relax and try and enjoy herself. I must live in the present, she repeats to herself, the new mantra, make each day count because I've said good-bye to the past. I've left it behind. As long as I remember I'm acting everything will be all right. Barry will protect me.

Barry has a history of being a generous host to hitchhikers and stray women from overseas who happen to be passing through, but his skills with the ladies are limited. In common with most of his countrymen Barry prefers the company of other males and encounters that won't tie him down, the archetypal giant who relies on his masculinity to paper over the cracks in his confidence, and who's secretly proud of his beard. When no one else is around he strokes it up and down, sideways and across, as if to confirm it's part of him. But Barry the bear has no intention of protecting Veronica because as far as he's concerned there's no need. She's tall, a good-looking woman, if a bit on the shy side, a good listener too, the kind of girl he likes to meet. He's looking forward to showing her his town, and she can obviously look after herself; how else has she ended up on the Coast, and a solo traveller at that. He's done a quick calculation – she must be about twenty-eight he reckons, and she's not hanging around so no risk of becoming a nuisance either. 'Bet I'm right,' he says with a grin as they set off. 'Come on. I won't tell anyone.'

Veronica/Julia says how did you know? A new name, and now a new age, all in the space of 48 hours. Her confidence returns, boosted by the surprising powers of invention. And it's true; when she's someone else she feels doubly protected, doubly safe. If she's asked what she does she'll say she's in academic publishing, as safe an answer as any.

Up and down the unremarkable main street they go, with Barry pointing out the modest landmarks until they get to a building down an alley with a painted sign announcing it's a pub. He leads her around to a side door instead of the front and raps smartly, twice, ratatat-tatting with his knuckles. Is it a secret code she wonders? Apparently so, because the door is opened and an arm appears beckoning them inside.

The room is large and badly lit, and the fug is a shock after the clean brisk air outside. A handful of men and women are already there, mostly sitting at tables with jugs of beer in front of them, 'Thirty-six ounces,' Barry informs her as he works the room, pumping hands, slapping men on the back as if he's known them all their lives, and introducing Julia/Veronica to all and sundry, telling them she's from England and they'd better behave themselves. He's obviously a regular. As for Julia, it's her first time in a real Kiwi pub. She resists the memories of the last one she was in, a night she has vowed to forget.

A lean man is pointed out as the local cop. 'Police officer,'

Barry explains aside. 'Off-duty.' Off duty or not, what is a policeman doing breaking the law, Julia wonders. She's confused. She knew Westport was small, but she didn't know it was lawless as well. The law-breaking policeman is nursing a beer like everyone else and talking to a middle-aged man with grey hair curling beneath his bald patch. Broken glasses sit askew on his nose, and one of the arms has been crudely reattached to the frame with a strip of pink sticking plaster. 'Ken, the town lawyer,' Barry adds. Ken likes an audience, especially someone he can instruct in Westland ways. 'Call me Ken,' he insists when they are introduced before Barry returns to the bar to pick up another jug.

CallMeKen is a fount of information and likes to show off a bit, especially when he has an attractive captive audience. But there's one thing Ken never shows off about, a piece of information that he keeps deadly secret. For Ken is a Baronet, a Sir. All thanks to a bachelor uncle who died alone and unloved in Penzance. In England Ken's title and profession guaranteed loans from his bank manager and lines of credit with the bookies. But when the debts rocketed out of control and the creditors started coming after him, Ken decided it was time he made himself scarce, time to do a runner and make a new start. In Westport Ken's secrets are safe, and if the gambling catches up with him again he'll move on and make a fresh start somewhere else.

Two women sitting together in another corner give Julia quick glances of assessment before relaxing back into their conversation. Their faces are tough, weather-beaten, and they hold their cigarettes like sixth fingers as they methodically down their beers glass for glass. Barry nods towards them expansively. 'They're sisters, twins actually, the pub's owners. They also run it as a hotel. Like their dad did before them. The bedrooms are upstairs, at the back. Pretty basic in fact, but what else can you expect. That's Westport for you.'

Barry suggests they get something to eat before the local

chippy closes so off they go, back up the main street to the other side of town. The same place as the one she went to the night before with Renate and Sigrid, the same smell of cooking fat and saveloys, and they join the queue. It's Friday night, fish and chips night. A drunken man lurches against her, knocking her off balance, and Barry steps in. She is afraid for a moment that there may be a real live fight, that she will find herself the centre of attention, caught between two men trading punches over her like a scene from a film. But Barry knows the offender, Barry seems to know everyone, and the drunk says he's sorry with elaborate mimicry. The school feels a long way away and the whitebait fritters Barry orders exceed their reputation. No resemblance to English whitebait at all. Tiny worms turned white by the heat with baleful pinhead eyes. But she's nervous again, unsettled by the drunken man, wondering what comes next?

In fact not much. Barry likes her OK, but he's still annoyed that she seemed to take a fancy to Ken. Just because Ken's a lawyer he thinks, even if only a small town one with a wife stuck at home. Barry finds it convenient to forget he's also got a stay-at-home wife, the one he left in Christchurch three years ago with their two small children. All because the second kid looked the spitting image of his best mate. Correction, his ex-best mate. Barry the man child.

Instead he says he'll walk her back to the boarding house and when they reach the corner he moves to kiss her. Show Ken a thing or two. But when it comes down to it Julia flinches and turns her head aside, because in truth she will never say yes to Barry, never let his weight pin her to a mattress or allow his beard to smother her face and her eyelids, never permit his large hands to force her legs apart. One day she may learn to trust herself again but until then this encounter is a canyon, not a bridge, the old nightmares a lurking barrier.

So she tells Barry that she feels terrible – headachy and fluey, too much beer. She's not used to it, and is off to bed with a couple of aspirin. Her face, tense and drawn, makes the lame excuses credible. Barry scratches his beard, his eyes crinkled with just the right amount of concern, his flattened nose tilted sideways in sympathy because he's actually quite relieved, albeit more stirred than he likes to admit. Only the first try he says to himself, a bit of a challenge. At least she's not a slag, and besides, there's plenty more fish in the sea. He's off rabbiting in the morning, but he'll pick her up again tomorrow night, same time same place. Julia doesn't know whether to be flattered or not as she says yes, she'll be fine by then.

She reflects that she's probably notched up more firsts in the course of a single day than she has in a lifetime. The thought makes her look at Barry again as he walks away, wondering fleetingly whether to call him back. Barry would be surprised if he could read her mind. And maybe a bit alarmed too. He'd be even more alarmed if he knew of her past. But that's the beauty of being a stranger in a strange place. The only past she needs is the one she is free to invent.

When he says goodnight, calling her Veronica, she catches herself looking round to see who he's talking to before remembering, and thinks of Luisa and the conversations they'd had, laughing about Luisa's lost virginity, with her pretending to be so worldly when she's not.

But Julia is already to move on, to leave Westport behind – too isolated, too small, too much of a community. Too much contact, too much Barry. Next stop Nelson. She's back on a bus heading north the following day.

As for Barry, years later a dipping helicopter blade catches him as he's helping load up deer carcasses. The hillside is steep and a sudden updraft catches the pilot unawares. Barry's head is separated from his neck in one clean sweep.

When the undertaker's job is done it's hard to tell Barry's head and body were ever apart. The magnificent beard, by now streaked with grey, hides the join.

CHAPTER 18

Nelson

It's a much shorter bus ride this time, less than half a day. The rain helps drive her decision. The forecast is for more rain, and more, for at least a week. Non-stop. In the wettest parts of the Coast, Ken had told her, the annual rainfall tops 400 inches a year, sustaining the forest, drip-dripping from trees and creepers and the drooping fern fronds, pattering down on to the mosses and lichens that carpet the forest floor. But it also obliterates the shadows starved of the sunlight that creates them, inducing an all-enveloping gloom, damp-ridden and oppressive. It can get a man down.

The Nelson climate's different, Ken emphasised, before launching into an explanation of the weather's behaviour on the opposing sides of the main divide – another term to absorb, the range of alps which form the backbone of the South Island. Nelson, land of potters, orchards, and fledgling vineyards that within a few short decades will become the mainspring of the province's economy. Alongside fishing and, one day, mussel farming. Ropes and ropes of them slung across inlets and the mouths of sheltered coves burrowed into the shorelines of the Marlborough Sounds. With luck she'll find work there, maybe apple picking, or in another hotel.

The bus is half empty. She's relieved to have a seat to herself, to be able to take stock, to examine whether she's managing to throw off the old nervous querulousness, to keep the enemy at bay. She'll stick with the job in publishing but add proof reading. If she stayed with academic publishing she'd be hard put to expand in the event of meeting a real academic. Keep it simple, keep it safe.

The Nelson hostel she finds is noticeably smarter than the Westport boarding house, and its homely feel and orderly segregated rooms invite a longer stay. By the end of the first week of apple picking she has blistered fingers and an aching back, and already doubts if she will ever want to eat another apple in her life. Most of the other seasonal workers come from Australia. The accent is similar, but different. She learns to tell the two apart after giving unintended offence. The rest are Luisas and Jorges, Carmens and Robertos, on extended working holidays from Chile and Argentina, a couple from Holland – Luuk and Emma, and two brothers from Greece. She's on a working holiday too, she contributes around the meal breaks and lounge-room conversations. But she's already tired of Veronica and decides to return to Julia. She never cared for Veronica in any case – V for vapid, vacuous, virgin. Julia is better – J for justice, joy, jeopardy. Anything but an A – angst, anger, apples; and never anything beginning with B. On through the alphabet, all the way to Zed, an alternative to counting sheep,

Along the row from her is August. They signed on at the same time and have had to learn to pick apples together. It's harder than it looks, and the less they pick the less they get paid. She adopts the same penny-pinching caution as the others to disguise her lack of concern with money matters; it's a luxury she can afford thanks to the tenants her parents have found for the Huddersfield flat. They've had to accept what she's doing because they don't have a choice. In exchange she's promised to write to them at least once a month. It could be the best thing that happened, they reassure each other. At least no one's forcing her, and there's been no more mention of 'that man'. If they avoid using his name perhaps he will disappear from their lives for good and the obligations tied to falling in with his wishes will dissolve, leaving the family at peace, able to square their consciences and recover on their own.

August is from England, like her, but from the South East. August's parents have a large orchard in Kent, but this is the first time she has picked apples at this level. Before it was just windfalls or the odd basketful. One by one, straight from the tree. Simple.

August misses her horse and her family in that order. Julia listens to August's hitchhiking adventures and can see why she stays safe, why she hasn't been raped or murdered. August is blessed with a face utterly without guile – open, frank, and serene, eyes untroubled, the embodiment of arrested innocence. She's taking a year out from a veterinary assistant's course near Newmarket. If she does well enough she may even apply for vet school.

Julia is back in the land of choices too, immersed in the Julia-renewal project. Up the two women go, up and down and back again along the rows, steadying their aluminium step ladders, tipping the red and russet-coloured apples carefully into carts hitched on to Enid Blyton tractors, avoiding bruising them, and talk and talk, about aching muscles and blistered hands, how good a shower feels at the end of the day, which parts of New Zealand to see next, and whether it's safe to hitch-hike alone. Or rather, August does. Julia as ever mostly listens, and when she does talk she carries on with the fiction of working for an academic publishing company. In the space of an hour she graduates from secretary to proof reader after her discerning eye for detail and typos attracted an editor's attention. An anodyne backdrop that dodges examination. It's too neutral, and questions are soon exhausted by the limited range of possible answers. Unlike working in a circus but better than saying she's a bookkeeper. It's a story that is adequate, fit for purpose, competently stifling questions as intended, giving away nothing at all.

Julia's strategy for survival proceeds hand in hand with her growing capacity for self protection. She avoids contingent experiences that could remind her of where she came from in the same way that she shuns the old upright piano in the hostel's lounge, the one with the ivory peeling away from the keys and the moth-eaten felts. Even if it were in tune and had no missing notes she would still avoid it. She never talks about music, or teaching. Not a word. She's taken a knife to her history which is now reframed as BB and AB, amputated. Whether it will return, growing back like a lizard's tail or some malign tumour, only time will tell. BB – before Britten, AB – after Britten.

Julia and August are soon joining forces after work and going off to pubs together along with 'the boys'. All men are boys now, and a boy/man is the accepted passport to pub entry. Just like in England. The first time Julia asks August's new friend Adrian to get her a tomato juice the barman is suspicious. His drinkers drink beer, proper drink he mutters. Adrian points to Julia. 'For my sister.' The barman grunts and asks how much vodka.

'No, not a Bloody Mary, just a plain tomato juice.'

Nelson's not so far from the Coast after all.

Adrian is a local, born, bred and educated in the town, and apple picking at some of the same orchards. He's studying law at Canterbury. Adrian asks August and Julia what they are doing at the weekend, whether they can get two days off together? He's going with a couple of friends to a family bach one of his friends has in the Sounds. The fruit picking season is nearly over.

'You can only get there by boat,' he adds, 'No roads at all, but if you haven't been to the Sounds you haven't been to Nelson.'

On the Saturday morning they meet him at the wharf early as arranged, together with a silent fellow student called Duncan, waiting to start the outboard engine and cast off. The sun is shining and the sea is calm for the hour-long boat ride, just little waves tilting against each other, the merest hint of white spray on their shifting crests. The boat is carrying food and drink for two days, and fuel and paraffin. Julia decides it's time to become twenty-seven if asked, if only to bridge the age gap. Or maybe twenty-six. No one doubts this claim by the tall pale woman with good bone structure, short strawberry blonde hair, and a vulnerability that makes people feel safe, unthreatened. Julia's self-effacement and gentle passivity have become her most powerful assets – that and the edge of mystery that surrounds her like an aura. August may be the younger, but that's not the way it seems. Julia is August's flotsam, drifting in her wake.

The bays they pass are dotted with small, often shabby houses, 'baches', Adrian corrects, tucked in against the dense green bush that cascades down to the water's edge, each house with its own jetty extending into the sea like a mini marina. When they arrive another boat is already tied up, signalling the other group has arrived ahead of them.

A battered cottage with peeling white walls and a dark green door faces them, perched on rough-cast concrete foundations on the bush side of the narrow beach's granular golden sand, for all the world like an elderly proprietor, looking out imperturbably as if assessing its visitors. Modest, unencumbered with telephone or electrical wires, sufficient unto itself. Inside the main room a pair of ancient brown leather sofas lined up against two of the walls face a wooden table made of rough-sawn planks and assorted chairs that have seen better days. Beyond the table a door opens into a galley kitchen with a wood-fired range and aluminium sink, the single tap fed from a rainwater tank perched on a platform outside. A rubber tube leads from a blue gas canister underneath the sink to a small cooking tripod. Battered saucepans stacked one inside the other stand on a sawn tree stump by the table, and a couple of frying pans hang from hooks beside a rusted horseshoe.

Two more rooms with bunk beds bear witness to the bach's role as a holiday getaway. The stand-alone WC is a short walk along a fern-lined path into the bush beyond. Yellowed squares, cut from the pages of old telephone directories and threaded onto a piece of string attached to a hook, make do for lavatory paper. The door, its top half punctuated by a cut-out heart, shelters a bucket of sawdust and a trowel. There is a strong smell of long-drop disinfectant.

The holiday history of successive owners and their families is piled into another shed propped to one side of the main building – a small dinghy and a canoe, oars, fishing rods, gaffs, billies, faded life jackets, flippers, snorkels and masks, a couple of saws and an axe, rusting paraffin lamps, sacks of kindling and, surprisingly, a set of boules. Neat brown wekas the size of bantams mince along the outside, picking their big feet up daintily, heads bob-bobbing from side to side, eyes alert for anything that shines. A bottle cap is seized and spirited away – weka booty.

That evening the eight of them – the other four came in on the boat that docked earlier, enjoy a meal of sausages, baked potatoes, chocolate, beer and more beer, and scallops Adrian and Duncan dived for earlier, scooping them up from the floor of the sea off the jetty. They are all tired, in a good way, from swimming, from a walk to the next bay and back again, taking turns with a machete to slash aside the barbed bush lawyer that snags clothes and rips at skin, accompanied by the trills of tuis and the plangent notes of bellbirds, their olive green plumage blending perfectly with the greenery. As the sun sinks over the horizon the daytime birdsong falls quiet and the sounds of the bush at night take over. The piercing calls of a kiwi and the mournful cries of moreporks seeking a mate mingle with the rhythmic surge of the waves as the tide comes in.

Sitting on the warmed beach beneath the Milky Way, the group gaze up at the Southern Cross and the other constellations – Orion's Belt, Ursa Major, Cassiopeia, the Big Dipper, discuss star signs and the way the Southern hemisphere stars differ from the Northern hemisphere, pop another beer, swap information about work, what jobs are going, and talk about future plans before drifting off to their bunks with their sleeping bags. Two of them are thinking of staying over for the winter, getting work in Queenstown, maybe on the ski field. Coronet Peak. A shooting star streaks across the sky, and then another – brief flashes of cosmic magic. 'Scintillate scintillate diminutive asteroid,' someone murmers. Twinkle twinkle little star.

Ever the good listener, Julia remembers to keep it simple, keep it safe, and sticks to academic publishing and a working holiday.

Time to go out on the boats, they agree the next morning after bacon and eggs. Peter is the son of one of the families who own the bach, and takes the lead. He's supremely confident, handling the boat like someone who's spent their whole life at the helm. The bach has been a holiday home ever since he was little and for Peter a boat is like a second car. So the outboards start up with a cough and a splutter and a burst of blue smoke, and off the two boats go. Another fine day, and in the bay they power ahead, hulls knock-knocking against the waves that slap against the sides, the wind unfurling hair and the prows dashing spray up into the air and across upturned faces.

When they get to the outer reaches of the bay Adrian turns back, because the boat is small, and the waves are always much bigger on the open sea beyond the headland. Julia is nervous, relieved when Adrian turns the wheel ready to return to the safety of the beach. But for some reason Peter carries on. Afterwards he will be unable to explain why, although one of his passengers remembers him saying, 'And now I'll show you what you should never do.'

So on Peter's boat goes, and suddenly the waves are bigger, and Peter realises he's made a mistake and wrenches the wheel around, too quickly, and the boat goes up on its side, propeller screaming as it lifts up out of the water, and out go his three passengers, flipped into the air like dummies. Only Peter is left on board, clinging to the wheel, using his weight as desperate ballast to stop the boat from turning over completely, hitting the Off button just in time. The other three are bobbing helplessly, shocked, buoyed up by the lifejackets.

Adrian and the others hear the screams and Adrian turns his boat around, powering back towards the scene. Spray spews up from the bow and the acceleration whips hair and faces. The next moment August, Duncan and Julia are grabbing arms, feet, shoulders, hands, heaving the casualties back on board, first one leg over the side, then the other, as the deck rocks beneath their feet and fingers grip the sides. People trip over each other in the confusion while Peter babbles excuses no one believes. Everyone is panting, breathless, Julia too – she's excited, gripped with the drama, feeling alive as never before until she notices that Ashley, the youngest, is injured. She cannot move her left arm. Her face is drained, green, and she's shaking uncontrollably. Julia helps transfer Ashley into Peter's boat where there's more room and joins her, holding Ashley's hand, wrapping a towel around her shoulders, providing words of comfort, of reassurance. With her other hand she reaches out to Peter. He's huddled behind the wheel, looking more alone than she can bear.

As it turns out, it's a good thing August is a vet, or a would-be one. She takes control, examining Ashley's arm and shoulder, confirming that the damage is in all likelihood torn ligaments or a sprain. She suspects a broken arm above the elbow, but keeps the thought to herself. It's important to keep Ashley calm, to avoid alarming her unnecessarily. In the bach she produces a first aid kit from her pack and fashions a sling from a couple of tea towels after giving Ashley two strong pain killers. Inside the bag Julia spots bandages, sticking plasters, pain relievers, disinfectant, even a suturing kit. The bach itself offers little more than a packet of ancient sticking plasters and insect repellent, and some clotted calamine lotion in a brown glass bottle with a cork stopper. Be prepared – August must have been a girl guide.

Everyone agrees it's only by sheer good fortune that the outcome wasn't much worse, but Peter's credibility is shot, his bravado and empty entitlement exposed. Adrian takes charge along with August who says Ashley must go to the hospital and be checked out, and her arm x-rayed in case there is a fracture after all. Sobered by their brush with disaster the two groups pack up for the trip back to Nelson the way they came, Ashley nursing her arm in its makeshift sling and wincing with every wave.

Julia sits by August, silent, keeping her thoughts to herself. The adrenalin has stopped pumping, and she's now consumed with questions. What if the engine's propeller had hit Ashley – she has a nightmare vision of the sea turning scarlet, of blood pumping out into the water from sliced muscles and flaps of torn skin. Ashley could have died, a critical artery could have been cut open, making her bleed to death. Life has never felt more precious.

Later on the aftershock catches up with her and she spends the night tossing from side to side as sleep evades her and she replays the accident over and over in her mind, trying to make up her mind what to do next.

She thinks of the £10.00 migrants on the boat out, the on-the-cheap hopefuls who clustered together, apart from the other passengers, bound by an invisible alchemy of mutual recognition. Were they escaping from an old life too, or escaping from themselves; did they really believe that by coming to a new country they would become new people? And of all the other emigrants who return within two years, hopes shattered, dreams broken, fantasies never fulfilled. The Whinging Poms who probably never had a chance anyway because of who they were, not who they could become, who thought a change of geography could bring about a change of identity, who will forever blame the country, the environment, the system, anything but themselves for faults they can never recognize, and never fix. Whose faces become etched with perpetual bitterness as the sylvan future they seek forever eludes them, receding further and further with each pointless step forwards.

As dawn breaks she drifts off to a restless sleep.

Dear Mother and Father,

I'm sorry it's been so long since you heard from me. This is just to let you know that I'm fit and well and happy, happier I think than I've ever been. I've been travelling around having adventures, some of them good, others not so good, but I feel so much better and believe I've done the right thing in deciding to see more of New Zealand and get away from everything. It's like starting a new life. I doubt you'd even recognize me now.

So far I've worked as a chambermaid and apple picker, and I've met fellow workers from all parts of the world – South America, Australia, Europe. I suppose you would call it casual work, or seasonal work, but there's plenty of it at this time of the year, and it's the perfect way to explore this beautiful country. It's also the kind of change I needed. I don't know why I didn't think of it before.

Here it's autumn, and soon the first frosts will start to appear. I'm writing this from Nelson where it's coming towards the end of the fruit season. If you look for it on a map you'll find it up near the top. After here I'm thinking of going north, all the way to Auckland, where it'll be warmer, especially with winter coming on, just as you're all looking forward to summer. I'll let you know how it goes.

In the meantime please don't have any worries: I am FINE, and safe, and enjoying every day. It was definitely the right decision leaving the school. It was tying me to my past and to memories that I need to forget, and I was getting unhappier by the day. Remember I came out here to make a new start. That's just what I'm doing at last.

Mother, you mentioned in your letter that father's been a bit unwell with a cough you said that won't go away. I hope the tests go well and that it's nothing serious. Let me know.

I'll write again soon.
Love, Julia

There's only one more week of fruit picking – apples, and pears, bullet-hard to keep in cool store and last through the winter as they are trickled into the shops. August is leaving for Australia. She intends to take a diving course on Kangaroo Island.

'Why Kangaroo Island?' Julia wants to know, 'And why diving?' She's in the course of making her own plans too.

'Barrier reef,' replies August as if it were obvious. Julia is impressed – diving means sharks. It sounds dangerous. She feels a stab of envy, wishes she could be more adventurous too, but she's learning, she's making progress. Kangaroo Island also happens to be home to marsupials, August adds, and other sub-species found nowhere else because it separated from the mainland 10,000 years ago.

Then there's the Tasmanian Devil, '…a kind of marsupial dog with a pouch.' She pats her pouchless stomach. 'And the duck-billed platypus. And the spiny echidna.'

August is already well on her way to becoming obsessed with Australian wildlife and showing signs of an unattractive didactic streak. Her confidence has been riding high since the day of the accident, nudging her innocence out of the way, and her ambitions are expanding. The wish list becomes longer by the day. Fired up with enthusiasm, she can't wait to leave.

'Besides, if I can get a job working in one of the kangaroo sanctuaries as well, or with koala bears, it should help me become a zoo vet one day.'

'Why don't you come too?' she suggests. But Julia replies no. She liked August more before the accident and by now she's tired of playing second fiddle. She's heard that Auckland is the best place to see out New Zealand winters so that's where she's headed next. She's feeling stronger for having faced down the shock of the accident, for coming through unscathed.

On her last day she joins her friends for a final night out in the pub, and Adrian buys the first round. The x-ray showed Ashley had fractured her ulna.

She'll be in plaster for a few more weeks. They all take turns adding their names to Ashley's by now grubby cast. Peter had to report the accident and it looks as if he may face a hefty fine that his parents will probably pay. But he's no longer so cocksure and Adrian thinks he's learnt his lesson. Adrian puts his arm around August and gives her a squeeze. August and Adrian have become an item.

Then it's off to the bus station and a complicated journey to Lyttleton to catch the ferry for Wellington, and from there another all-day bus journey north. Julia has already discovered that it's easy getting work if you're white, have an English accent, say you're prepared to do pretty much anything, and don't argue about the wages. And it definitely helps to lie about your age. The younger the better. She'll go to a city hostel and take things from there.

As the ferry approaches Wellington harbour the vicious wind that sweeps the narrow strait between the country's two main islands attacks the boat with a ferocity that triggers an outpouring of seasickness. Wan passengers, their brows beaded with sweat, stagger against the sides of the lurching corridors and gangways, and soon the decks of the aging vessel are awash with vomit. Berthing looks like an impossibility. But the captain's voice over the speakers is reassuring. Windy Wellington he explains. They'll wait a couple of hours until the wind eases and try again. This time they are successful.

Another night in another hostel before she's on her way again, rising at dawn, stopping briefly at towns swathed in geothermal vapours, looking out from her seat on the near side of the coach on improbable green hillocks and mile upon mile of bush, on gingered sawmills and swirling rivers, past invisible rats, stoats, weasels, feral cats, possums and a myriad ravaged birds' nests, looking forward to being in a city again after months in the backblocks and small provincial towns of this strange country.

Five years later Peter is found hanging from a tree behind the lean-to at the bach after his girlfriend dies from preeclampsia, his final day of life reduced to a cliché, another bereft statistic pinned to a list that lengthens by the month. He had said he would marry her but she'd turned him down, saying one baby was enough. Psychologists are starting to become concerned about rising suicide rates amongst young white males in God's Own Country. Godzone.

And August sends her a Wish You Were Here postcard from Australia where she's been joined by Adrian. As intended, she finds out all about koalas before becoming a fully qualified veterinarian and working in the zoo. Their children grow up sharing the house with baby animals abandoned by captive mothers. Even when they've left home they will remember the hourly bottle-feeding schedules that disrupted their sleep, sidelined by small furry creatures that outstripped them in loveability.

CHAPTER 19

Auckland

She's at the university, studying the student union notice board. Someone at the youth hostel has told her students often advertise for flatmates there, and Auckland's youth hostel is too expensive for a long time stay. And different too – nothing like other hostels she's been in, and she doesn't like it. Too busy, too noisy, and not enough privacy. It's all very well being twenty-six, but when you're actually thirty-three it becomes a strain living the younger life and matching shared reference points.

Most of all she's missing a room of her own and desperate to find one. She's aware that the old anger is still there, anger dating back to her time at the hospital and all the previous times when she was discounted, treated as a nobody. Yesterday it almost broke through the boundaries she's erected with such care.

The usual youth hostel bore had been boring on and on, non-stop, self-absorbed, impervious to his impact on others, his nasal American accent penetrating every corner of the communal lounge and the corridors beyond. First of all it was about hunting and the guns he owns back home in Wyoming, and how many elk he's killed and how many more he's going to kill right here in New Zealand. Boy, if he could find a bison he'd kill that too, Holy Cow. Make the horns into one helluva helmet, the skin into a rug that would cover a wall. On and on and on. A wishful Custer in love with the sound of his own voice, impervious to others, a would-be killing machine, a pint-sized bully adrift in a host country, seeking always to compensate for his lack of height by elevating his ego instead. Yes, he's all pumped up, a Remington 8 on legs. Ready to go.

He's still not finished. He's never finished. Now he's braying on about all the places he's visited. Julia wonders why he hasn't been murdered yet, and her anger starts to boil inside her. Is no one going to stop him? She looks at his mouth opening and shutting, spewing out an endless torrent of words, the jug ears and deep-set wounded eyes, the snub noise and crew cut, the high Irish colouring and the cheeks with the blue-tinged stubble line. Then sees the man for who he is. It's another moment of empathy that saves her from exploding. Instead she intuits the infant's ego beneath the bombast, the foundling forever looking for a home that doesn't exist, and her anger fades away. But it was a close thing – that's why she has to find a room of her own.

Years later Duane O'hanlon, for that's his name, has his legs blown off below the knee by a landmine in Vietnam. He gets new ones made of metal and plastic, and becomes a motivational speaker, sustained by an imperative to talk that never deserts him, nor leaves him in peace.

Memories of the women and children he shot and the villages he helped torch fester beneath the professional bonhomie until the day he dies.

While Julia is getting ready to meet with unknown Adam, the student who's advertised the room, the composer's lawyer is dialling a number. He has news for his client, and has thought hard about how to deliver it. He looks at the letter again, the one from the headmistress of the school in New Zealand, headed In Confidence.

He is aware he should have called sooner, much sooner. After all, months have gone by, but it was easier to procrastinate.

The news was hardly unexpected. Indeed, it had always been a possibility, given the issues at stake. He doubts there's anything he could have done in any case apart from letting the composer know. In essence the woman had disappeared, giving no formal notice, leaving no forwarding address. But a subsequent letter from her to the school had proved she was still alive. There had been fears she may have done something rash, something irrevocable, euphemisms the lawyer assumes for suicide.

The headmistress added that the teacher never settled into her post and had difficulty imposing discipline. The remit was clearly beyond her. The tone is more sorrowful than reproachful. We all did our best, she continued in her spidery handwriting, but the unfortunate woman clearly had problems we couldn't fix. 'She left abruptly so we contacted the police in case something untoward had happened.'

The subtext is clear; the woman had suffered another breakdown of sorts, but the school could no longer accept responsibility for her. 'If she asks to resume her post again I will let you know.'

A year later the new headmistress also resigns, to be replaced by a tall disciplinarian who wears a constant scowl of disapproval tempered by an unhealthy relationship with alcohol. Like the music teacher, the English headmistress had also failed to impose herself, an innate reserve finding her wanting, her inexperience and weaknesses laid bare one by one, month after month, term by term. Her elderly mother, who can no longer remember her name, dies on the voyage back and is buried at sea.

The composer answers the phone, his hello sharpened by anxiety. The call is unexpected and he's immediately on guard.

But it's all rather inconclusive. The lawyer explains the situation, relaying what limited information he has, and points out that since there were no contractual obligations governing where she could live, there's really nothing that can be done. On the brighter side she appears to be safe. There have been no reports of any accidents or encounters with the authorities, and her departure from the school could be taken as a sign that she's better, and getting over her obsession. The self-serving rationale is quickly accepted. The woman is still 12,000 miles away and it seems inconceivable that she will be returning to England any time soon. A modern-day remittance woman indeed.

The composer remains disturbed however, because it's back to the unknown. He asks the lawyer to let him know if he hears any further news, and to contact her family and check, discreetly, whether they have heard from her or know what her intentions are. They will need to be approached tactfully – a general enquiry into her well-being, and see what that elicits. The brother duly confirms that yes, she's written to her parents and assured them she's well, and staying on in New Zealand for an indefinite period to see the country. Apparently she was unhappy at the school but sounds cheerful now. There's no mention of any return of the mental problems.

The information is relayed back, and the composer relaxes and puts the news out of his mind. Work has never been busier or more absorbing. Tippett and Vaughan Williams are snapping at his heels. He frets that his music is falling out of fashion, and scours the critics to see who is in the ascendency. Ever competitive, it is essential that he keeps on creating new works and he's already embarked on his next opera, this time with full orchestra. Peter is spending more and more time at their London home for some reason. And then there are the first signs of a heart problem too, possibly damaged by that long-ago attack of childhood pneumonia. Arrhythmia the specialist said. When he wants to restore some sense of perspective he casts his mind back to the appalling scenes he wishes he could forget – the concerts he gave with Yehudi Menuhin to concentration camp survivors just after the war. Bergen-Belsen was the worst of all.

Adam is a surprise when Julia meets him at the university café – not the young student she'd been expecting but a thirty-something PhD candidate in a field vaguely connected with social sciences. A small leprechaun of a man with a snub nose, and hazel eyes that gleam with intelligence. From certain angles he looks uncannily like Lenin. All that's missing is the cap.

For Adam, Julia is part of an informal experiment he's conducting, but he has no intention of letting her know. That's part of the experiment too, and Adam hopes to mine it for material for his doctorate. Adam fancies himself as an intellectual, a left wing iconoclast and latter-day existentialist in the tradition of Sartre and Camus. He tells her about the four-bedroom house he rents off the Parnell Road, and says two of the other tenants have just left, hence the vacancy. She can have the bigger room if she likes although it will naturally cost a bit more. Is Julia interested? The house is furnished, and even has a garden. The location could hardly be better. And does she like cats?

Julia says she'll come and see it the next day, after work. Yes, she's found a job almost straight away, cleaning work at a motel up near the top of the road. She's one of a team of eight and has been partnered with Scottish Angela, the pretty wife of a science teacher, from Edinburgh like her, at one of the city's premier schools. The information doesn't stack up; why is shy Angela doing a low-status poorly paid job if that's the case. Over the coming weeks she will find out a great deal more, not just about Angela, but about the other cleaning women as well.

When she arrives at the address Adam gave her, she sees it's another traditional New Zealand bungalow, probably dating from the beginning of the century – old for this country – with the usual corrugated iron roof painted a rusting red, cream weatherboard walls dusted with cobwebs, and matching windows like secretive eyes. The kind of house a child would draw.

A concrete path with crumbling edges leads from the steep pavement down to the front door, beyond it a hallway with two bedrooms either side, then the bathroom and a big kitchen, propped up on posts above a basement area tucked into the slope of the land as it falls away to the bottom of the garden at the rear. Thickets of blackberry, and trailing vines of squash and convolvulus and blue-flowered morning glory grow rampant over long-neglected flowerbeds, stimulated by the sun-drenched aspect and the city's sub-tropical climate. A couple of depressed-looking rose bushes, their leaves disfigured with black spot, vie for the remaining space.

The other flatmates include one of Adam's university friends – a woman called Viola whose cultivated eccentricity is her defining feature, and another, much younger student who replied to the same vacancy notice as Julia. Four of them all told. And the cat, Adam reminds her, a large intact tabby who belongs, it seems, to no one but himself and who is relaxed, friendly, and infinitely sociable. His frayed collar reads Adam too, but he's been renamed Trevor to avoid any confusion, and disburses his favours evenly and without prejudice, occupying each bed in turn and leaving early in the mornings, as discreetly as a lover.

Trevor seems the most balanced occupant of them all. Tensions appear almost immediately. Tony confesses it's his first time away from home. He's nineteen, still with a face like a baby's. At the end of the first week Adam is prompted by Julia to ask Tony why he's letting his dirty dishes pile up by the sink, day after day, encrusted with blobs of congealed egg yolk, unwashed, attracting large black flies that buzz like hornets. Tony looks surprised. He didn't think about them he says. Why would he?

His mother always did the washing up for him. Julia wonders how he got into university in the first place. Tony for his part looks wounded. Hurt and offended. The Bambi eyes well up with unshed tears. He's not one to join the dots. Adam shows him how it's done and explains the benefits of washing up liquid.

Secretly Adam is delighted – his experiment is already yielding results. He just has to find a way of framing them. When a dead mouse, desiccated as a mummy, is discovered in a shelf corner behind a rusting tin of white pepper, Adam watches, gauging the reactions. Late at night he writes up his notebook before locking it away in his desk and putting the key back on the gold chain around his neck, next to the large greenstone tiki that hangs there like a talisman. The disparate household he has brought together is already challenging assumptions about non-familial relationships and what happens when strangers separated by age and nationality are brought together in forced proximity, suggesting a whole new field of research. Adam's practical experiment in social engineering sits comfortably alongside his own appetite for control and a secret desire for a two-seater performance car. The end justifies the means, he reminds himself in a nod to Machiavelli, regardless of awkward ethical niceties like consent, or transparency.

Interesting too that Julia called upon him to act as intermediary, raising issues of ownership and deference, avoidance versus confrontation. He needs to do more research on personality types and examine, even revise, extant definitions. Grist to the mill for the thesis that will one day form the core of a widely praised postdoc research paper on team building theory, only diminished by missing attributions and the background he inaccurately assigns to her. For Adam under-estimates Julia. When she said she helped her parents manage the family hotel in a town called Huddersfield, he took her at face value. He'll look it up on the map when he finds the time.

Academic publishing is no longer an occupation she can hide behind: too close to home when mixing with students, and especially someone who probably intends to get into print one day. But she can guarantee he knows nothing about Huddersfield and even less than she does about working in a hotel. Besides, she can always draw upon her Hermitage experience to plug any gaps. After all if it was good enough to get her the job at the Gateway Motel it should be good enough for Adam.

She takes the same route to work every day, fifteen minutes up the street, through the park entrance with its tall metal gates, past the rose beds that look down on the harbour and the curling jigsaw inlets, past a group of tree ferns, and past the Elf – an eccentric park fixture in his long skirts and matching shirts, and as friendly as Trevor. He waves her a cheery good morning from the bench he's always sitting on as if he's known her all his life. Sometimes he beckons her over, and if she's running early she stops for a chat about nothing very much. Small talk, the weather, flowers, bees and how hard worker bees work, how they find their way back to the hive, how they communicate with each other. Elf has read Carl von Frisch and is a fount of bee knowledge. It's a reassuring start to the day before she puts on her work overalls and joins Angela, or maybe Kate today, or Eve, and begins making beds and envelope-tucking the corners, changing towels and scouring the copper-bottomed saucepans in the kitchenettes, or doing a complete clean when the occupants have checked out. Sharing the tut-tuts at the signs of a rule-breaching party – empty bottles, beer cans, bulging wastepaper baskets, towels thrown anyhow on the bathroom floor. Sometimes a used condom under a chair or spatters of vomit around the lavatory bowl. And once a huge pool of congealed blood when she peeled back the bedclothes to make a bed.

She was on her own that day, and quickly pulled the sheets up again, leaving the blood untouched. Let the occupant complain if she dares, but nothing happens at all, just as she calculated. She knows who the culprit is, a woman in her sixties, smartly dressed too, on her own. It's hard to imagine the cause of so much blood given the woman's age, and why the woman is still capable of walking around as if nothing untoward has happened at all. Other people's secrets: everyone has them. Hidden, impenetrable, often shameful. The job may require her to clean up vomit, but not this.

The next day she's assigned the same room, this time with fifty-something Eve who screams, her hand over her mouth, eyebrows disappearing into her hairline in a parody of a horror movie, and changes everything. Julia pretends to share Eve's shock and leaves her to make up the bed again on her own while she gives the saucepans a superfluous extra shine.

Then Mary comes round to inspect the rooms and satisfy herself that the sparkling units meet her exacting standards. Mary started like Eve and the others before she became the supervisor. She has a natural authority that fits her for her role, and is rumoured to hoover and dust her own home every day when she gets back from work. Julia is a bit in awe of Mary, who she thinks could do any job if she wished to, but Mary is happy being the master of her small kingdom rather than a minnow in a bigger one.

Julia thinks this is the most relaxing job she's ever had in her life, even more relaxing than the work at the Hermitage – round and round, same old same, limited demands, limited responsibilities, interspersed with unexpected dramas that pop up like treats.

One couple, a sweet old pair well into their seventies, become friends. Friends of everyone. They have been staying in the motel for two months, and even Mary likes them. So kind, so considerate, so devoted to each other. Then one day they're not there. Nothing – empty room, car disappeared, and an outstanding bill that's never paid. Mr and Mrs Sweet Old Couple have done a runner. A police check on the car's number plate shows it's a fake. The SOC are clearly practised confidence tricksters. Yet it's hard to summon up much indignation. After all, they are simply doing what everyone else would like to if they had the nerve, Julia reasons. Mr P, the motel's owner, is the only person who's genuinely exercised by the deception. 'How could they!' he snorts. 'They were OLD.'

And some days are in fact very different, like the day Mr P turns up asking who can speak French. Julia puts up a tentative hand; only schoolgirl French she ventures, but that's enough for Mr P. Two French people – from PARIS – are staying for three nights he announces, and he'd like to take them out on his new boat for a sail around the harbour. Mr P fancies himself a cosmopolitan sophisticate, even if he doesn't speak French, and likes a bit of showing off. The motel business is booming, and besides, what's the use of money if you don't spend it. Show people you've got it. Julia accosts the middle-aged pair who look alarmed. What have they done wrong? Until they eventually understand she's extending an invitation, not a summons.

Julia's stock as a woman who can speak French rises and Mr P struts away, congratulating himself on his largesse and diplomatic skills. The day is a resounding success, bright and sunny, with just the right amount of wind, a triumph for a Parnell/Paris entente cordiale until the unfortunate *Rainbow Warrior* episode years later. He returns the couple at the end of the day, Jean-Pierre and Madeleine by now, and tucks the jaunty captain's hat under his arm, gaily calling out Au Revoir. If he had a string of onions he would twirl them round his neck, or swing a baguette over his shoulder, and no doubt whistle a few bars of the Marseillaise for good measure if he could only remember the tune. On the drive back to his house in up-market Remuera he decides to order a Breton top. Perhaps one for the wife as well.

Angela's is the next drama. It all comes out in an article in the newspaper, a shock horror piece that has aspirant parents of privileged teenage boys reeling in indignation. Angela's teacher husband has been exposed as a charlatan. He's not a qualified chemistry teacher at all. In fact he doesn't even have a degree. How come he was employed by the school in the first place? Didn't anybody think to check up on the bogus degree, or his references? Why hadn't the other teachers listened to the sixth-formers' suspicions, aroused by his apparent inability to come up with answers unless he'd taken a quick break.

Julia thinks he would have made a good accomplice for the SOC, but Angela, already a diffident, subdued personality, is reduced to virtual invisibility by the shame and unexpected notoriety. Instead of staying at home and taking a few days off, she comes in earlier than the others and leaves later: the motel is her sanctuary until reporters stop besieging her home and move onto another story. The husband is charged on some unspecified grounds and the school is left to deal with the fallout, its reputational complacency terminally punctured.

Julia wants to keep this job for as long as possible. She's finally at peace, comfortable in her own skin at last, and has spare time to boot that Adam helps her fill. He's often waiting, casually, in the kitchen when she gets back, eating a late sandwich, friendly, too plain, too asexual, too short to be a threat, with polite enquiries about how her day has been, what her work mates are like, an anodyne interest that allows her to sink back into comforting passivity. If someone were to sit her down at a piano she doubts she would be able to find middle C.

For his part Adam treats this as part of his research, and he's curious to see what happens between Julia and Viola – polar opposites, and therefore full of potential for his project. Will Viola reveal herself as a patronising bully, will Julia resist, push back, or will the two women collude in some secret women's compact to ignore each other. So far they seem to have barely registered each other's presence. Finding Julia was like pinning a tail on a donkey, blending chance and calculation in equal measure, but he's already sensed that she is essentially unknowable.

Unlike Viola who is a queen bee, surrounded by acolytes she collects and brings back to bask in the privilege of her company. Viola selects her audiences carefully, avoiding competition, and would like to reign over a salon one day, blending talent and promise to complement her self-appointed flair and outré opinions.

Viola's persona is carefully cultivated, but her disdain for others is entirely natural. Likewise her condescension, driven by an earnest desire to distance herself as far as possible from her parents' struggling dairy farm and their servile respect for authority. Young men in pairs, wearing cheap suits and dark ties, patiently court them with monthly visits and talk of Armageddon.

Viola likes to identify herself with the emerging beat generation. She plans to go to San Francisco as soon as she's finished her Masters. Or better still, New Mexico. Drink tequila and swallow the worm.

Creating this persona has been hard work. Viola is as conscientious about populating her expanding book collection as the most committed librarian, her bookshelves as carefully curated as a shop window. Titles by Marcuse, Wittgenstein, Adorno, jostle for space alongside the cluttered cosmetics on her bedroom table, the worn sticks of kohl and the eccentric wardrobe – Indian saris, embroidered waistcoats. The rewards are measured by the reputation she's acquired on campus and the stares she attracts in the streets. She's already weighing up the advantages and disadvantages of having an affair with the new Philosophy lecturer, assessing the pros and cons. He's going places the word has it in the department, and she's seen the way he looks at her. He has a weekly radio slot and was interviewed by *The Listener*. She just has to flick a beckoning finger. Creating future networks, future obligations.

Tony and Julia are quickly categorised as minor players she can ignore, Tony too young and callow, Julia too invisible. Julia for her part views Viola's studiously acquired uniqueness and her arresting clothes as just that – so much attention seeking, but at the same time admires the ambition that has gone into constructing such a calculated identity. Unlike her own efforts which have been all about effacing herself and her past. Viola's casual dismissal when Adam introduced them is proof of her success.

Nonetheless she cannot help enjoying a satisfying moment of schadenfreude the day she sees Viola's self-regard falter in the face of events no one could have foreseen.

It starts off as an evening like any other: Adam is in his room writing, the light tenor twang of Woody Guthrie seeping through the thin partition walls into the passageway. Tony is still at the university library, finishing an assignment. Julia has finished a late supper of a cheese sandwich with rubbery processed ham. When the door opens she assumes it's Viola, and so it is, but this time with her friend Dicky. And Dicky is looking very dicky indeed – blood all over his face, nose swollen and clearly broken, and a large cut across his left eye. Viola is propping him up as he staggers in, clutching his left side in pain.

Julia jumps up when she sees them. What happened? And where is Viola's usual lofty composure? Who is this frightened woman calling for help and covered with her friend's blood, face blotched with shock? Well, Dicky is Viola's friend and comes round often, and it turns out he's been queer-bashed. Yes, beaten up, queer-bashed. Just down the road. On the way here. Three of them. One punched him in the face, then the other. And then all three kicked him on the ground, grunting abuse with each blow – queen, faggot, pooftah, queer, and Viola jumping up and down, screaming on the sidelines. They are both shocked – how could this happen in Parnell? Parnell, with its alternative life-style vibe, gentle folk singing clubs, and left wing activists committed to human rights and stopping American imperialism

Adam wants to call an ambulance but Dicky says no. Emphatically. He's adamant, he'll take a taxi to the hospital instead. Julie hopes the driver won't be put off by Dicky's blood messing his clean seats. Viola stays with Dicky as he leaves, still holding wads of tissue to his battered face. His swollen eye beneath the cut is already turning purple.

After they've left with the grumbling driver Adam joins Julia in the kitchen and asks her if she's OK. His show of concern as he waits for her answer lacks conviction, and Julia's intuition is right. Adam is excited rather than concerned. He asks Julia whether she has 'connected' with the situation, whether she's shocked, frightened, whether she knew Dicky was gay, whether this happens in England too.

Julia replies with her usual practised platitudes, unlike Tony who is aghast when he hears about the attack and wrings his hands in distress. Viola returns from the hospital around midnight, her cheeks still streaked with mascara, saying Dicky's got a broken nose but thank goodness the eye socket is undamaged. A couple of cracked ribs will make laughing uncomfortable for about six weeks and reconstructive surgery is lined up to restore his good looks. The incident has been reported to the police. Viola looks exhausted, drained by the attack on Dicky and her own inability to prevent it. She will sign up for a self-defence class. Otherwise she fears she will be forever listening to the footsteps behind her, crossing roads, clutching house keys, seeking out street lights.

But the night hasn't ended yet. As if Dicky's being beaten up weren't enough. At two o'clock – Julia remembers checking her watch, there is a loud banging on the door again. Bang bang bang. She hears Adam stumble down the passage. Viola's door opens too. It's started raining outside, heavily, and she can see the raindrops backlit by the street lights as they hiss down and splash the path in wetly glittering bursts. A girl is standing in the doorway, clutching her belly, a girl with short blonde hair – late teens Julia guesses – and wearing nothing but a stained brassiere and underpants, and a pair of filthy sandshoes with missing laces. She's been raped, the girl gasps. Adam opens the door wider, pulling her in.

The girl crouches down on the floor moaning and writhing, and no one knows what to do. Water runs from her hair, down her face, pooling on the floor. Then the girl says she's pregnant, and going into labour. Viola could never make an entry like this. She's outclassed, comprehensively. Moreover, the girl has a trim belly as flat as a pancake.

More material for Adam's notebook, but he's been thrown into panic mode. For a moment the detached observer Adam is replaced by a dithering man who doesn't know what to do. 'We should call social services, or an ambulance,' Julia states bluntly. It's abundantly clear that the girl needs help, professional help as well as shelter, and no one present knows this better than she does. They are not remotely qualified to deal with the situation, and they're deluded if they think they can. But no, Adam replies. 'Absolutely NO.' By now he's recovered his poise and is as adamant as Dicky was previously. The very notion offends every tenet he holds about authority and personal freedom.

'If we call social services the police will come and she'll be taken away and locked up. We must take responsibility for her ourselves. The girl can stay the night in my bedroom, where she'll be safe.'

'We'll look after you' he promises her, 'until the morning.' His eyes gleam with the drama. Real life, literally on his doorstep.

So Adam gives up his bed to the poor soaking girl with the crazy eyes and no clothes, and produces an expensive sleeping bag.

But even then the night still isn't over. A couple of hours

later – by now it's nearly 4am, Julia is woken again by another wild rumpus in the passage outside. Peering out of her bedroom she sees Adam and the girl locked in a tug-of-war at the open front door, she at one end of his sleeping bag, Adam at the other. The rain is still cascading down, the drops falling in silver diagonals, shimmering threads like diamonds, a bizarre surrealism out of some Gothic horror. Adam wins – after all he's a man, even if a small one, and therefore the stronger, and staggers back with the sleeping bag still intact, and still his. The girl bolts athletically down the path and disappears into the sodden night, still in her underpants with one of Adam's sweaters over her top, and is never seen again.

Adam is puffed, red in the face from the effort, chest heaving. His hair stands on end, exposing the high temples that betray his early onset baldness. Adam doesn't mind about the sweater. 'It was the sleeping bag that was valuable,' he explains. 'Top of the range, goose down,' then realises he's said something that only a capitalist would say. Ooops. Adam's socialist tenets and advocacy of collective ownership have been found wanting at the first real test. Just like his idealism. Trumped by pragmatism.

As for the exhausted Viola, she's encountered someone beyond her experience. The night's events and her helplessness when Dicky was attacked have exposed the cracks, forcing her to ask if she is in truth a beta, not an alpha. And now this. She's diminished in consequence, her self-confidence punctured, deflated like a week-old balloon. Her wish to be at the forefront hides the fact that she's fundamentally a follower, not a leader, guided by polarity, not principal.

Adam, by contrast, from his mid-thirties vantage point soon puts the experience behind him, insulated by the fact that he knows exactly who he is – popular, venal, ambitious, manipulative, likeable, smart, intelligent (two very different things) and self-serving, the ideal qualities for where he's heading, where he's going. He may not be good-looking but he has charisma. The baldness adds to his authenticity. In his notebook he writes that he told the girl she could keep his sleeping bag. Because he cared.

And in time he will recast the story of the girl until he's convinced that yes, he really did let her take his sleeping bag, just as the notebook says. Adam may be adept at interrogating events; less so when it comes to interrogating himself.

Julia alone is strangely unaffected, detached even. The calm after the storm. She's been there herself, survived bouts of ECT and therapy, hit rock bottom and come out the other end. Granted she raged against her treatment at the time, the way it reduced her to a zombie, and just pretended she was better. Anything in fact to secure her release. But short of telling Adam her history, how else could she have persuaded him to listen to her. Hopefully the girl has friends, family, who know she is missing and will look for her. After all, doesn't everyone have a family.

Back in Julia's room Trevor stretches lazily on the bed he's suddenly got to himself, back arched, tabby legs extended and big yellow canines showing in a yawn before he burrows back again into the warm bedclothes. His whiskers twitch happily and his pink tongue flickers before he resumes a dream involving chicken scraps snatched off plates, and saucers of creamy milk left out as a tribute to his feline charms. The flea powder Adam had dusted him with has done its work and he's enjoying his first good night's sleep in weeks.

The most extraordinary evening two days ago – a girl, a complete stranger, turned up here in the middle of the night screaming nonsense and clearly having an acute mental episode. But nobody called for professional help or thought of getting an ambulance to take her to a hospital for an assessment, or calling social services. And in the end she disappeared just like she had come, into the pouring rain in the early hours of the morning. What were they thinking of. Are they really so stupid or so immature.

Or were they right, and it was all fake, pretend. No, that's impossible. Something was very very wrong.

The worst thing is that I couldn't insist on getting help without letting them suspect that I had 'personal experience'. I mentioned it, but Adam and Viola dismissed my suggestion out of hand. They seem to share a left wing distrust of authority, so I just stood on the sidelines and watched. It's complicated and I'm confused myself. It's difficult even writing about this.

Actually I think they're both embarrassed now, and secretly realise their response was wholly inadequate but refuse to admit it. So I've decided to stay silent and keep my views to myself. Tony I can understand because he's only a boy. But Adam is older and should know better. How could he have been so careless about a sick girl's welfare, and so unbelievably arrogant.

They are already making it sound like an amusing adventure when they talk about it with their friends, and any meaningful discussion about what happened, or what other actions they could or should have taken, seems off limits. The only amusing thing was seeing Adam leap into action when he thought he was going to lose his precious sleeping bag. But this was tragic, not funny. One day it could be them.

As for myself, I have no intention of ever going back there or becoming a curiosity for Adam to examine, so I haven't raised the subject again either. I see him watching me sometimes and I know he takes notes about what he likes to call 'group dynamics'. He thinks I don't notice but I do, and I need him to go on thinking I'm ordinary, not like the girl. I cannot afford to let other people label me based on something that happened before I came here. Otherwise what am I doing here in the first place?

Nonetheless I keep on remembering how distressed she was, how 'mad' if I can use that word, and still wonder what happened to her. I seem to be the only one. Maybe she was on drugs, in which case she should definitely have been taken to hospital. It certainly looked like a full-blown psychotic episode. But Adam insisted. So was I a coward? Should I have insisted too? Actually even if I had I don't think he would have taken any notice

We all have secrets and I wasn't prepared to share mine, not even for the girl.

I hope she's safe, and that someone is looking after her.

CHAPTER 20

Burger time

Julia decides she needs to find an extra job. The motel one leaves her free from mid-afternoons on with time on her hands. She ponders her options as she walks back through the park, waving to the Elf who's wearing a different batik today – hibiscus pink, blues and oranges, and a scarf wound round his head like a turban. The splendid effect is undermined by the spindly white legs and incongruous pointed brogues, but Elf doesn't care about irrelevant details. He's much more interested in showing her his new sunglasses with their purple frames. Julia hopes he doesn't get beaten up too but decides against warning him. She doesn't want to spoil his day.

The rose bushes behind his usual bench have been pruned almost to the ground for winter and the ink-green Norfolk Island pines stand up like beacons, as geometric as trig stations, branches akimbo. Evergreen native trees and shrubs with names she cannot spell or pronounce fill the gullies at the edge of the fall-away lawns, and balls of lime-green grapefruit hang from a clump of energetic citrus trees clustered together on a sunny spot further up the hill, making the most of the city's semi-tropical climate, so different from the cold and brisk frosts of the south. She's decided to stay on in Auckland as long as possible. An evening job will be ideal.

Which is how she finds herself flipping burgers at a mobile burger bar down the road the next week alongside Gary.

Vaughan, or is it Vernon, is the manager, and Gary's bête noir. Vaughan has a habit of dropping by without warning on random evenings at close of business, just to keep an eye on things he says. Gary needs to do more than just serve the food, Vaughan is always complaining. He must look like food too. Gary struggles to get it. What's Vaughan talking about, what's he really trying to say?

'I shouldn't have to explain,' Vaughan replies irritably as he looks over the takings. 'You either have it or you don't.'

Gary needs the work. He assures Vaughan that he does have it, he just has to discover whatever 'it' is. Julia watches; she is an accomplished people watcher now and enjoys it more than she can ever explain. Other people's lives.

Gary grumbles about Vaughan behind his back and Julia listens, absorbing his disgruntlement, helping damp it down just by listening, nodding her head, looking sympathetic, saying nothing, and getting on with the work. The striped apron and matching hat suit her. It's a shame the same can't be said for Gary. Perhaps that's the problem. It's hard to look like a food ambassador when wearing a hat that makes him look absurd regardless of his Pat Boone good looks and the thick brown hair that falls across his forehead like a curtain. Maybe that's what the elusive 'it' is all about – a simple change of hat.

But there's nothing wrong with his burger flipping skills and the way he tosses onion rings around the wide metal sheet, or slaps the burgers onto the baps with a flourish, adding a practised squirt of tomato sauce for good measure. Or cracks open eggs with one hand like a chef, sunny side up, easy over, over easy, whatever the customer wants. Julia thinks that if Vaughan could see Gary in action his concerns would vanish. Custom is brisk for the first few hours, then falls away as the night lengthens. At around 10pm Gary says it's time for cleaning up and drifts off to have a cigarette.

But first they prepare their own hamburger supper; it may sound like the same thing every night but soon Julia and Gary are making an art of it, aiming for the perfect, the definitive hamburger experience. How many squirts of sauce? Onions browned or see-though opaque, or just a tiny bit burnt to add a tang of bitterness? Yellow mustard all over, or just a dab in the middle? Or around the edges only? Baps browned, or just warmed up? Two burgers or one? Rare, medium rare, well done, charred, or burnt to a crisp?

If you put your mind to it there's room for limitless invention the two burger cooks discover, and before long Julia's bringing extras too, like squares of processed cheese, slices of cucumber. They create a ratings list using percentages – 70 per cent is adequate, anything over 90 is excellent, and 100 per cent is impossible, a reach for the sky aspiration they can never allow themselves to achieve, because then the hunt for the perfect burger will have to stop. They agree there's no such thing in any case, not with the cheap processed mince Vaughan buys in bulk, pressed into flat discs that curl at the edges, and where price trumps quality. But even burger making requires ambition if it's to be worth the grease, the smell, and the endless repetition, so the game continues.

Once the perfect burgers are eaten and out of the way Julia scrapes down the cooking plate with an instrument like a blade, and collects the leftover fat and grease into a kind of drain, or gutter, before wiping everything clean, putting away the leftover burgers in the fridge and wrapping up leftover baps, leftover lettuce, leftover onion rings. Wiping off the smears around the necks of the bottles of ketchup and bright yellow mustard ready for the next day.

Until she arrived on the scene Gary had to do all this himself. It was only when he threatened to leave that Vaughan agreed to extra help. No wonder Gary likes Julia so much – in a strictly professional way of course, not his type. Unlike his girlfriend who is curvy and tanned and sloe-eyed, small enough for him to scoop up in his arms and squeeze tight when they're laughing behind the sand dunes.

The nicotine in his cigarettes has never tasted so good as he fills his lungs with long drags on the tobacco, flexing the tension from his shoulders, looking up at the stars and thinking about the cosmos before helping Julia with the final cleaning details and locking up, the end of another burger shift, the end of another day.

There was the small matter of the holdup too, but he's decided not to tell Julia about it. No point in making her nervous. He's still nervous himself to tell the truth, and still resentful that Vaughan at first seemed to think he was on the fiddle, that it never happened, that he'd pocketed the takings himself. Instead he walks her back home at the end of the shifts. It's only a few minutes out of his way he says, and besides, it's a way of thanking her for taking charge of the scrag end of the day and the cleaning up.

Gary's been doing the job for eight months now and wants to do something different so he doesn't always smell of burger fat and fried onions. The smell sticks to his hair, his hands, his clothes. No amount of washing seems to get rid of it. Something will turn up – he just doesn't know what it is yet.

Listening to him, Julia shares his viewpoint. After all, ever since she left the school something has always turned up for her too, and so far it's been all good, every something another step along the path to recovery. The crazy girl was a yardstick. Remembering her theatrical groaning as she writhed on the floor, Julia appreciates yet again how far she's come.

So they carry on, rubbing along together companionably,

a team no less, until it happens again. The same two youths, pimpled foreheads above the concealing scarves, a pair of jittery racoons, knives trembling in shaking hands, demanding money again. Why the hamburger van though? The amount of money they will get is pathetic, custom has fallen off with the colder weather, and it's going to be closed for the next two months anyway, part of the winter break. Julia feels like advising them to try somewhere else, somewhere worth the effort. Gary shrugs, and hands the money over – a few pounds, shillings and pence, the coins lying limply in the bottom of the cashbox as if apologising for their scarcity.

When the young bandits see what they're getting they swear and throw the box on the ground before waving their knives again under Julia and Gary's faces in a show of bravado and running off into the dark to chase down some random Plan B. Vaughan is cross when he hears about the holdup, but that's all. Julia says the money is safe because Gary was brave and refused to hand it over. Gary keeps quiet, but gives Julia a quick nod of gratitude. They're a team. Gary may not look like food but he's happy to pretend he's a hero. What better way to end their hamburger partnership.

Yet another first Julia says to herself – the list becomes longer and longer. Only in New Zealand she thinks, and only because she has been able to cast off her past, to leave it comprehensively behind. But what of her future? Time to start thinking about that as well because if she's certain of one thing now it's that yes, she does indeed have a future.

Dear Parents,

It's spring here now. Strange to think it's autumn in England, and that the trees will soon start changing colour. I'm still in Auckland, which is much hotter and more humid than the South Island, and in many ways almost tropical. Lemon trees grow in ordinary gardens, next door to roses, and grapefruit trees too.

Of course lots of things about New Zealand are like England, but in other ways it really is another country, especially when it comes to the plants and the bush, and unlike Australia no snakes either. You should think of coming out here one day, maybe miss the English winter.

At present I'm still working on the reception desk in a hotel, and am enjoying it. The manager has said I can stay on longer if I would like to which is probably a good idea as it would see me through to the end of the year and give me time to decide what to do next. I've also been helping out at a restaurant, and have done some waitressing, which has been quite a change. I found the job through my flat mate who is also English, out here on a working holiday too, so we have plenty in common and often take bus rides together to see more of the surrounding areas and the countryside.

Auckland definitely feels more like a city than anywhere else I've been to in New Zealand, and the harbour is in easy walking distance. The other weekend we also caught the ferry to Waiheke Island only a couple of hours away. Even though it's so close to the city it is still very undeveloped with the usual dusty shingle roads and holiday houses. I think that's the thing I miss most about England – the tarsealed roads. Certainly not the climate. And of course everyone is friendly and welcoming. I've also met quite a few people from the university as well as I'm living in a very 'studenty' part of town, and the university campus is near by.

Thank you in the meantime for looking after the flat and

sorting out the new tenants. I'm glad you found an agent to take it off your hands. The rental money is a great help. So as you can see you don't have to worry about me. At present I have no plans to return to England. I'm happy and well, and the work suits me much more than teaching.

Your daughter, Julia

PS I hope father is feeling better and that the doctors have given him the all clear.

Let me know what the specialist says.

In the aftermath of the encounter with the girl who turned up in the middle of the night, Viola is briefly consumed by a passing interest in mental health issues before going on to become a feminist, committed to activism. *The Female Eunuch* joins the titles accumulating on the crowded bookshelves, alongside Betty Friedan, Joan Dideon, Erica Jong, Mary Shelley. The list is exhaustive, and she decides she's a lesbian. Her shoulder-length locks are shorn off and replaced by a crew cut that flatters her long neck and delicate jawline, perversely making her look more feminine.

After she gets her Masters she applies to UCLA in the hope of completing a PhD, but the costs are prohibitive. Instead, she ends up with a junior lectureship in women's studies at a small state university in Ontario where she lives with a succession of partners. The saris are swapped for jeans and boots and a swagger, hands in pockets. A doctor informs her that recurrent bouts of gonorrhoea have left her infertile, ever the forerunner, ever chasing the vanguard, until age and dementia reduce her options to zero.

And Adam? Well, Adam starts a left-wing magazine and acquires a stake in a bookshop. The timing is right, the venture aligning perfectly with the zeitgeist of the 60s, and turnover is brisk. He introduces literary nights: once a month, when the shop has closed for the day, authors read their newly published books to rapt student audiences sitting on the floor, legs crossed in front of them, knees bunched up, faces tilted to attention, and established New Zealand poets and not-so-established poets recite their poems. The atmosphere is extremely earnest, even when the poems are humorous and the novels comedic. New Zealanders are at the beginning of a quest for cultural identity and this is a serious business indeed. Soon 'home' will mean New Zealand, not England, and the country's cinema audiences will stop standing up for God Save the Queen at the beginning of screenings and start learning the words of God Defend New Zealand instead.

Over it all Adam presides, his baldness and domed forehead validating his growing renown as something of a local guru, a networker and facilitator it pays to be on the right side of. A thinker and a shaper. His research paper was called inspirational, cutting edge, when it came out. His subsequent papers on team psychology and transactional dynamics morph into a management tool adopted by business schools worldwide.

He also pays an undisclosed sum for the two-seater sports car he always yearned for, making sure it's a vintage one, a connoisseur's rarity. It is shipped out from California, cocooned in a customized crate, burdened with a welter of paperwork and chrome accoutrements that gleam like platinum.

Only Adam and his accountant know how much he's earning.

He'd have preferred the new E-type Jag, just out, dark green like the Norfolk pines in the park, but that would have been too ostentatious, too flashy for the image he has constructed so carefully. As carefully in his way as Viola in hers.

And when the English magazine *Granta* is relaunched in the late 70s, Adam quietly assumes some credit for showing how it could be done.

CHAPTER 20

Return

Dear Mother,

I think your letter must have crossed with mine. Let's use airmail in future. As you can see I'm writing on an aerogramme because it's so much quicker than surface mail.

Poor father, what a shock for you both. You say it's too late to operate. Are you quite sure? Have you had a second opinion? Of course I will come home, and hope I can manage it as soon as possible. I'm going into town this afternoon to speak to a travel agent about booking a place on one of the sailings and will write again once this has been arranged to let you know when I expect to be back in England. Most boats dock at Tilbury, in which case I'll then take a train from London.

In the meantime I'll try and call you on the telephone. It's complicated of course because apparently I will need to book a slot and then let you know when, and sort out the best time given the time differences. I'll try and find out from the post office how it's done. Maybe it will be best if I send you a telegram once the phone call has been agreed. I think it costs about a pound a minute, so we will need to think about what we want to say first.

Tell father I'm very sorry to hear he's not well, and look forward to seeing him again. It's been quite a long time I know, but time well spent. I don't think you would recognize the new me now as I really feel I've been able to put the past behind me and make a new life here.

*Your loving daughter,
Julia*

So now it's all hustle and bustle, telling Mary she has to go back to England because her father is terminally ill. But she hopes to return when it's all over. Mary steps forward to give her a hug. Julia recoils as tactfully as she can, pretending to be stepping back, pretending she missed the cue. Tactile is something she still shies away from. Angela oozes empathy. She knows all about pain. A dying father – she can scarcely bear to think about it. She loves her own father deeply, even more so since the separation, and doesn't know how she would have survived the last few months without him. Fortunately he's in excellent health.

Mr P says they'll be sorry to see her leave and to remember there's always a job waiting for her at the Gateway when or if she comes back. Would he say that if he knew about the bloodied sheet she refused to touch, she wonders? And she realises how much she'll miss them all, their generous acceptance of her, their kindness and lack of intrusive curiosity, secure in small lives embellished by the dramas that invest them with significance. Lives enriched by the modesty of their aspirations. She's doubly touched by the farewell gift Mary hands over, a pair of teaspoons with enamel ferns on the ends of the handles, and a New Zealand paua shell, rainbow-iridescent on the polished inside, gnarled on the outside, encrusted with the calcified traces of tiny marine hitch-hikers.

At the travel agent's down town in the city centre Julia makes a new best friend, Mr Ted Markham, who sits behind an old-fashioned wooden desk cluttered with brochures and Michelin guides, and piles of badly folded city maps. A disproportionately large map of the world is pinned up on the wall behind him, showing the countries that make up the sprawling British Empire, enduring evidence of mercantile self interest mixed with imperialism, executed with all the righteousness of force majeure, the reds disappearing one by one in surrender to self-rule imperatives.

The two and a half islands that comprise the sum total of New Zealand sit humbly at the bottom, almost hidden, dwarfed by their grander neighbours, sometimes left off maps altogether.

Mr Markham's eyes, owlish behind his glasses, glitter with enthusiasm beneath his tufted eyebrows. He could be discussing an entire round the world adventure instead of the one-way berth to England that Julia has requested, for Ted suffers from a compulsive desire to travel with his clients, albeit in imagination only, the ultimate vicarious explorer.

His trip two years ago to Italy with Mrs Markham is still as fresh in his memory as if it were yesterday. He would have preferred the Amazon, to have travelled into the unknown, a latter-day Livingstone, thrusting his way ahead of a dwindling retinue of loyal native bearers, machete in hand, slash swipe slash, struggling against malaria, teeth chattering, sustained by his bible and his faith, clasping Stanley's hand and doffing his topi, replying 'Yes, you presume correctly.'

But no matter. Rome turned out to be a gratifying substitute – Ted striding across the Colosseum's great arena, muscles rippling with exertion, sword in hand, the flailing opponent trapped in his net, looking to the emperor – Caesar, Augustus, Justinian, Nero, even Nero's horse, for the thumbs up or down signal, the crowds hammering on their shields, roaring their approbation. Ted as Androcles, Ted as Spartacus, Ted as Ted, the mightiest gladiator of them all.

Ted's wife despairs at times. How has she ended up married to a fifty-five year old Walter Mitty fantasist with a head stuffed full of dreams of adventures that will never happen. Who wakes her up at night mumbling place names she's never heard of and twitches in his sleep like a lurcher chasing a hare.

It's fortunate, she reminds herself, that Ted has essentially had to stay an armchair traveller only, sustained by little more than a faded geography degree and a vicarious relationship with the adventures he creates for his clients, constrained by family responsibilities and a stubbornly modest salary. Otherwise he may well have disappeared for ever, become a Tony Last figure held captive by a madman, erased in some fever-ridden corner of the Brazilian jungle. Malaria, leprosy, bilharzia, yellow fever. She pulls herself together with a jolt. God help me, she's starting to think like he does. Warning bells clang in her head, beware the slippery slope. Time to get up and put on the kettle, time for a nice cup of tea.

But it looks as if Julia isn't going to oblige so back to more prosaic things, like looking up schedules and options, and making Julia's reservations. Is she sure she wouldn't like a stopover in Aden Ted asks, as temptingly as a courtesan, or Suez, or Panama. Or Mexico. Or French Polynesia, Bora Bora – just a quick hop from Darwin. 'Or Easter Island, Rapa Nui. No? As you wish. Pity though to cross the world without taking the opportunity to see what's in between.' And a hopeful wildcard, 'Have you thought of Russia?'

Julia's firm: once she's explained why her plans have

to be immediate Ted – Mr Markham, is all sympathy and understanding. And reveals a newfound enthusiasm for air travel, the latest thing, becoming increasingly popular. So quick too! Besides, no need to endure any more tiresome Neptune celebrations and fancy-dress tridents as the boat crosses the Equator, or debilitating weeks of seasickness and deck quoits. Granted the seats may be on the mean side and the cabins as narrow and cramped as a cigar tube, but otherwise every comfort you can think of. Smiling stewardesses in smart court shoes and tailored uniforms at your beck and call, china plates, free drinks. And speed. What more could the traveller in a hurry wish for?

It will take less than five days he adds proudly, including refuelling stops and transfers on the way, and hey presto, he's found a flight leaving Auckland and then on to London in two weeks' time, and another the week after. Spoilt for choice.

Ted leans back in his chair with smile of modest triumph, a conjuror who has produced not one rabbit from a hat, but two. If she comes back next Wednesday he will have a draft itinerary ready for her. Then he can finalise the bookings. And tell her how much is costs, ha ha. Is that likely to present a problem? No she replies. Excellent, and will she be wanting travellers' cheques for the journey, just in case the plane is delayed en route. By bad weather perhaps. Or a missed transfer. He recommends Thomas Cook's. Apparently a plane was delayed in Capetown for a whole day recently when a tiger bound for a zoo in Germany tried to fight its way out of its transport crate and had to be tranquillised. You never can tell.

And finally, is she absolutely certain she wants a one-way ticket only? Regretfully Julia says yes, because she is not sure how long she will be staying in England. She intends coming back to New Zealand but she doesn't yet know when. It all depends. Her voice trails off, and Ted almost squeezes her hand in sympathy. Almost. Back in the Parnell Road house she checks the card in her wallet again, Edward Markham, Senior Travel Agent, and gives him a call. She's changed her mind. She wants an open return ticket after all.

What to do with her last few days? Say goodbye to the Elf, admire his newest batik, go the top of One Tree Hill and look down over the city, capture memories. Sitting at her mirror the following evening, Julia looks at her renewed reflection, the refreshed haircut and the new colour, a deep chestnut brown suggested by the hair dresser she went to on the spur of the moment after finalising the travel plans.

It's helping her fight down the doubts, quell the threatened panic attacks. Will her mother recognize her when she meets her at the station? She hopes not, afraid otherwise that her family will treat her as she used to be rather than who she has become, that she will be reduced by expectations that no longer apply. Another thought occurs to her – will she even recognize her father? What will she say to him? According to her mother's telephone call the doctor says it's only a matter of weeks. He's very thin, her mother warned and the radiation therapy had proved both futile and debilitating. Decisions, decisions. The bookings have been confirmed and the tickets issued – bundles of them, copies and copies, flimsy pieces of paper covered with flight numbers she can barely read, as illegible as a doctor's prescription.

Even Viola, quieter now, less arrogant, has been unexpectedly kind, as if noticing her for the first time, and compliments her on the new hair colour. It makes you look striking she says, beautiful in fact. Another first. Looking at the face looking back at her, Julia sees what Viola means.

Strange that her journey is going backwards now, back to its starting point, to where it all began. She prays that she won't find herself going backwards too, but is buoyed up by the last ten months, time she never anticipated, experiences she never imagined. A journey of healing and self discovery. The trip back to England will be another test, one that will prove she has killed the demons once and for all, emerged unscathed and purified from all the years of darkness and obsession, has found a life worth living – her life, not someone else's.

Dear Mother and Father,

I may see you before you get this as I've decided to come by air. It's much quicker and I've already bought the tickets. When I get to London I'll get a train up to Huddersfield, and call you ahead to let you know what time it gets in. I think I have to change at Birmingham. If you could arrange to meet me at the station that would be much appreciated. Otherwise I'll take a taxi.

I've sent a separate telegram with my flight arrival time.

It's all been rather rushed I know, but the travel agent here has been very helpful. It would have taken weeks to come by boat, and there weren't any departures for a while so I took his advice. It will be quite an adventure. I'll tell you all about it when I see you.

Thank you too for offering to let me stay in my old room. I will be tired when I arrive so please don't invite any one around until I've caught up with my sleep. I'm told that time differences can create problems with sleeping for several weeks, and that I could start dozing off in the middle of the day and waking in the early hours until my body clock adjusts.

I'll try and give you a telephone call as well before I leave next Wednesday, but have decided to send this letter in any case. I'm looking forward to seeing you and father, and again I was sorry to hear that the news wasn't as good as you must have hoped.

Your affectionate daughter,
Julia

CHAPTER 21

Homecoming

Julia doesn't want to think about the journey. It was long, just as she'd been warned, and her hair still smells of cigarettes. The efforts the other female passengers had put into dressing for the trip had been disconcerting, another surprise. The makeup and lipsticks, the long waits outside the dolls' house lavatories as vital cosmetic adjustments were made in preparation for landings, the elegant exits as studied as if the wheeled gangways were catwalks.

She reminds herself that she is an adult, a grown woman, not the twenty-something she's been masquerading as. The old Julia would have been the same as the other women on the plane she expects, unthinkingly subscribing to an unwitting conformity, but not the new one, not the new autonomous Julia with the short chestnut-brown hair, slim and androgynous, colouring clear and pale as a Renaissance madonna, dressed for casual comfort rather than an office or cocktail party, still reserved, but serene, self-sufficient, poised not anxious. Head held high.

For Julia has become deracinated, a triumph in itself. She gives a swift thanks to all the Adams and Marys, the Garys and Augusts, the Mr Ps and Luisas, all the men and women she has met over the past months who have helped her on her journey, made the new Julia possible. She even thanks the school, and the girl. But for her rejection Julia may never have taken the steps she did. Rock bottom – nowhere to go but up. Into the unknown. And it had worked

From the train going north she looks out at the rolling English landscape with its domesticated prettiness and gentle hills, on through the bleak industrial towns of the Midlands, over soaring viaducts, past the familiar cooling towers rearing up like monstrous megaliths, belching clouds of steam into the sky, and reflects on all the things in her life that have changed. The same language, but a different country from the one she's come from, a different people.

She is different too, but she is still fearful as the train gets closer and closer to her destination. Is she mentally strong enough to survive a return to her home town, however brief? Or will the old horrors return to seize hold of her mind and threaten her sanity again? She reassures herself with a quick glimpse at the complementary travel wallet Mr Markham had given her for her passport and itinerary, and by the wad of precious return tickets, passports to her future.

When the train pulls into Huddersfield after a swift transfer at Birmingham, she spots her mother on the platform, waiting anxiously, eyes scanning the passengers getting off, still searching as Julia walks toward her. Looking confused, wondering why her daughter hasn't appeared.

She's been so worried – about her husband, about Julia too in spite of the letters and assurances, unable to sleep for the worry. After all, she'd said farewell to a broken, fragile woman and she doesn't believe in miracles. How could she? The damage seemed too deep to ever be mended.

Accompanying all this is the abiding guilt that accompanies every parent's thoughts when their children's lives are not perfect, guilt that she wasn't a better mother, that she failed to recognize the girl's fragility in the first place. Had she been cruel, where did she go wrong, is the fault in herself – a failure of imagination, of ambition for a child's happiness? Settling for the default of good enough.

They had always recognized she was a reserved child, but never thought she would become morbidly so. Was helping her buy the flat indicative of selfishness rather than generosity, a convenient route out of parental responsibility? The answer has to be yes, and yes again. Looking deep inside herself she sees in hindsight that she and her dying husband gave their daughter everything except love. A difficult birth, a late third addition to the family, unplanned for, the secret vomiting they had been aware of but had chosen to ignore, the evidence of the obsession deliberately overlooked and denied.

And worst of all, allowing themselves to be bought by the offer of a ticket for their daughter to the other side of the world, effectively selling her. The thought of the transaction, the lawyer, the shame, continues to reproach her, making her look for a punishment. Like her husband's illness. Was that her fault too, the necessary price for absolution.

But where is she? People have been streaming past on their way to the station exit, suitcases in hand, and still no sight of her until a tall woman with short chestnut hair stops in front of her, and says with a polite smile, 'Hello mother'.

She stutters with surprise. Apparently miracles happen after all.

After the funeral Julia says she'll stay on for another week. Then return to New Zealand. Together the two women sort out her father's belongings, the usual by-now forlorn remains of a conventional life lived unremarkably, suits, jackets, shirts, pullovers, ties – too many, raincoats, olive-green water-proofs, all piled into cardboard boxes and taken to the nearest charity shop to be priced up with pieces of paper safety-pinned to sleeves and collars. Shoes, socks, and any other items too old or worn are put out for the rubbish collection and unused prescriptions returned to the chemist's. The son takes the golf clubs – the grandson will use them when he starts taking lessons. The older sister is happy to wait until it's her turn when their mother dies, the unspoken contract.

There is one surprise though, not such a great one perhaps, it happens with many families, but a surprise nonetheless – the bundle of used cheque books Julia finds at the very back of one of the drawers in his desk with an account number her mother doesn't recognize. The stubs show regular payments going back for years.

When the will is read the lawyer discloses a small bequest for another daughter, a half-sister it transpires. A secret life or romantic tryst, a side to her father no one knew about or thought possible. Had Julia treated him as a cypher too, she asks herself, failed to discern the person beneath the accountant's façade. Had the Lodge meetings been a cover for improbable assignations? Did the girl, or woman by now, come to the funeral unrecognized, unannounced; was she watching from behind a gravestone, hiding behind a yew tree; does she have a name, how old is she, who was the mother, should the family attempt to get in touch? More questions, questions. When will they ever go away? The consensus is no. If he chose to take his secret to the grave so be it. If he had wanted them to know he would have told them. Instead he left it to his lawyer, in the final analysis a coward. No need to broadcast a distant domestic transgression or make a fuss, they all agree. A very English family indeed.

Only the dog seems genuinely distressed, an elderly eczema-ridden poodle that whimpers quietly as it roams the house searching for its dead owner. Soon its time will come too when the vet conveniently puts it to sleep. Julia's mother can't help wondering why the same couldn't be done for her husband, why he had to linger on, slowly suffocating to death. Why animals are allowed to die without having to endure unspeakable pain, but humans are not.

Julia confirms flights for the return journey, her quiet confidence and evident self-sufficiency forestalling family questions about what she plans to do next. There's something almost intimidating about her now, a sense that she has left them behind when it had always been the other way round. The old neediness and social ineptitude were easier to deal with. The new assurance obliges them to ask uncomfortable questions of themselves in the knowledge that their paths are set, that it's too late to change course, to make other choices. Unlike Julia who seems to have found a different route leading to a high road they cannot follow, leaving them stranded in a present she no longer shares.

But first Julia has to do something she has thought long and hard about. To write another postcard to the composer. Her motives are obscure. Even she cannot read them. All she knows is that it's something she has to do. Like getting back on a horse that you've fallen off, diving back into the pool where you nearly drowned. Closure. Another burial. This time a fitting one.

But for the composer it's not so much a burial as a revival that he's been secretly dreading, that confirms his worst fears, fears he's been trying to ignore ever since the telephone call informing him she had left the school and disappeared. Fears she would come back one day, that the hideous drama would start all over again. And his stomach lurches with apprehension when he sees the envelope with the familiar handwriting waiting in the letterbox.

Like the previous ones he destroys the card, lighting the match, watching the edges catch fire and curl as the flame takes hold, blue at first, then orange, reducing the paper to blackened ash, the words still faintly visible on the charred fragments. It carried no signature but the telltale lettering was instantly recognizable – the same ink, the same familiar quotation: 'To love as we loved was to die, daily with anxiety; to love as we loved was to live on the edge of tragedy.'[17]

For the rest of his days he will find himself scanning audiences, haunted by an anxiety that lurks in his subconscious like an incubus, perpetually condemned to wonder if the woman who screamed out his name is somewhere out there, watching unseen, scheming, whether another stalker has replaced her, whether his new house is being watched by unseen eyes, whether he did the wrong thing, whether he will ever shed the doubts about his judgement, the guilt and the unease that refuse to go away.

It is early autumn, or late summer New Zealand time, almost eighteen months since she first arrived. Adam says he's giving up the lease on the house. He can afford a place of his own now. Would she like to take the lease over, become the responsible adult.

And Mr Markham is all agog when she remembers her promise to contact him on her return and takes the bus to his office to let him know how the travel arrangements went. What was the food like, did the transfers work, the other passengers, the aircraft, was it noisy, the different airports, the smell of the different countries, England?

Mr M is clearly getting itchy feet again, already caught up in embryonic plans for his most ambitions overseas trip yet. South America, land of the Incas, of Machu Picchu, the Conquistadores, Aztec temples, humming birds bright as jewels, cloud forests wreathed in mist, Perito Moreno, the Salar de Uyuni, Patagonia, the Drake Passage, Antarctica. For once turning dreams into reality. It all depends on Mrs Markham.

But he needs someone to keep an eye on his desk if he's going away. In fact he needs an assistant. He looks at Julia appraisingly – an experienced traveller by now, smart, English accent, mature enough (he's seen her passport), good looking, a good listener, and back in the city permanently she says.

Julia accepts the offer because frankly it's better than the motel, and Mr Markham carries on fine-tuning his itinerary in a controlled frenzy of excitement. She will work alongside Mr Markham, 'Ted' he insists, as his trainee over the next few months while he applies much needed discipline to his jumbled wish list and takes a course in Spanish. Maybe pen a travel book or two as well he thinks, *The Victims of Pelosi*, or *Rustling with the Gauchos*. Meanwhile Julia knuckles down to memorising alpha bravo charlie delta echo foxtrot, and learning how to become a travel agent.

And when she returns to the house on Parnell Road, this time as the new Adam, Trevor greets her as if she's never been away, rubbing himself against her legs, purring noisily as she sprinkles some more flea powder over the bald patch where his tail joins the rest of him, and pours another saucer of milk. Viola has already left for Canada after the UCLA disappointment but Tony is still there, in the second year of his engineering degree.

A friend of his moves in and the two young men drink beers in the garden and invite other friends around to cut back the blackberry and rip out the convolvulus. They light the barbeque with scrunched-up newspapers and many wasted matches, blow on the charcoal until it's glowing, and dance out of the way of the chasing smoke, vainly flapping at it with their hands, taking turns with the toasting fork and tongs before serving up sausages with exploded ends, folded in slices of soft white bread stained red with ketchup. And afterwards Tony and his friends clean everything up, put the barbeque back under the house, and wash the dirty dishes in the kitchen sink before drying them and putting them away.

His mother still does his laundry once a week when he brings it home, and irons unnecessary creases down the legs of his jeans. Adam's old room becomes the new communal sitting room.

She also starts playing the piano again, picking one up at the city auction house. Rosewood inlay with hollowed-out brass finials either end for candles, and an iron frame. Back in time to the baroque harmonies of Bach and Handel – no more modernists. The slow, measured, opening solo notes of Handel's organ concerto No 4 fill her room and float out the window. A passer-by stops in his tracks to listen. He thinks he's never heard anything so achingly beautiful.

THE END

Endnotes

1. Benjamin Britten, *Canticle 1, Op 24:* lyrics from *A Divine Rapture* by Francis Quarles, 1947.
2. *The Gospel of John*, 18: 13–27
3. Ronald Duncan, *Working with Britten – A Personal Memoir* (Rebel Press, 1981), p159.
4. Duncan sets these events in 1956, but I have settled for 1955 as the only year that fits the known facts.
5. Duncan, p134.
6. Duncan, p134.
7. Benjamin Britten, *The Rape of Lucretia*, libretto by Ronald Duncan, 1945.
8. Benjamin Britten, *Wedding Anthem, Op 46, 4th stanza*, text by Ronald Duncan, 1949
9. Britten, *Wedding Anthem*.
10. William Shakespeare, *A Midsummer Night's Dream*, Act 1, Scene 1.
11. Francis Quarles, *Canticles ii*, 16, Verse 1.
12. Duncan/Britten, *The Rape of Lucretia*, Act 1, Scene 1
13. Duncan/Britten, *The Rape of Lucretia*, Act 1, Scene 1.
14. Duncan/Britten, *The Rape of Lucretia*, Act 1, Scene 1.
15. Shakespeare, *A Midsummer Night's Dream*, Act 1, Scene 1.
16. Benjamin Britten, *Phaedra*, libretto from Robert Lowell's translation of Racine's Phèdre, 1975.
17. Duncan, *The Rape of Lucretia*, Act 1, Scene 1.